SHELBA SHELTON NIVENS

The Mistaken Heiress

HEARTSONG
PRESENTS

Recycling programs for this product may not exist in your area.

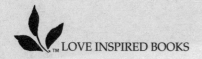

™ LOVE INSPIRED BOOKS

ISBN-13: 978-0-373-48707-3

THE MISTAKEN HEIRESS

Copyright © 2014 by Shelba Shelton Nivens

www.Harlequin.com

Printed in U.S.A.

"I'm sorry, I should have introduced myself."

She whirled away from him, crossing her arms as though to ward off his answer. "It doesn't matter to me in the least who you are. You won't be around here much longer."

He could tell by her stance that she was waiting for him to tell her anyway.

But he didn't. He could be just as stubborn as she. "Look, do you have time to walk over the property with me?"

She turned back to him, subdued. "It's beginning to look as though time may be all I do have—now."

"Ouch! You hit below the belt." He said it teasingly, but she kept her back ramrod straight and didn't return his smile.

He discarded the smile. "Shall we go for that walk now?"

She shrugged. "Sure. Why not?"

He grinned. *She's likely thinking she'll stick around long enough to discover what I'm doing here and how she might find a way to claim the place. And what harm will it do to let her try?*

SHELBA SHELTON NIVENS

is a community columnist for her county's newspaper, the *Shelby County Reporter.* A published playwright, she served for forty years in the drama ministry of her local church. Her book of local history and genealogy sells to individuals, history groups and libraries across the U.S., and is often quoted by other writers. Shelba and her husband, Ken, live in central Alabama on land settled by his ancestors. They have three children, six grandchildren and six great-grandchildren.

"For I know the plans I have for you," declares the Lord, "plans to prosper you and not to harm you, plans to give you hope and a future."
—*Jeremiah* 29:11

Chapter 1

Dust fogged up around Kate Sanderson's sneakers as she ran across the open field.

It was hot for Thanksgiving. She stopped in the middle of the dry garden patch to catch her breath and wipe her sweaty brow on the tail of her T-shirt.

Dropping her shirttail, she grimaced as she noticed, again, the brown stain on the front of the shirt. *I sure did it this time. Acted like a klutz in front of the whole family. And on my first day back.*

She turned to look at the large white house behind her, recalling her mother's stinging words at the dinner table. *For crying out loud, Kate. Will you never cease to embarrass me? Just look at that glob of cake on the front of your shirt.*

Everyone else had looked at the smear of chocolate, too. Kate shook her head and heaved a deep sigh as she thought about her family still sitting around the big oak table. Then, turning, she feasted her eyes on her sanctuary on the far side of the garden.

Tall pines swayed in a sudden breeze, their long green arms beckoning her. A smile touched her lips as she lifted the mass of tangled curls from her neck to let the fresh breath of air cool it.

Dropping her hair, she bent and pulled a dry pea vine from around her jean-clad legs. Then she struck out running again across the garden patch.

At an old familiar opening in the undergrowth, she stepped into the coolness of the forest.

Green pine trees interlaced branches with sweet gums, maples and poplars painted with the reds and golds of autumn. A shower of bright color rained down around her.

As Kate kicked her way through fallen leaves, her shoes stirred up an underlayer of long-decayed foliage, a musty reminder of autumns past. She had very likely tramped on many of these leaves when they were crisp and fresh from the trees.

Sadness slipped over her. Attempting to shake it off, she lifted her face to the breeze and kept walking. She wanted to see the old farmhouse again. She wanted— She stopped and sniffed the air. Did she smell wood smoke?

Fear gripped her as into her mind flashed the image of her beloved woodland in charred ruins. She turned to sniff in all directions. All she smelled was sun-warmed leaves and spicy pine needles.

Satisfied her nose had been playing tricks on her, she began moving again.

But at the edge of a clearing, she stopped short. Her mouth flew open. There *was* smoke in her forest. One thin, gray wisp curled lazily upward from the charred remains of a campfire.

Beside the fire, on an upturned piece of firewood standing against a pine tree, sat a man.

He held a coffee mug in one hand, an open book in the other. His hair and beard glistened blue-black in a streak of sunlight

She stared for a moment, transfixed. Then she noticed the tree. *Her* tree. The gnarled old oak in whose branches she had often sat to sketch and read.

Why, the nerve of him!

She was on him in a flash. "What are you doing here? How dare you hang your clothes on my trees and build fires on my land."

She snatched an offending garment from a limb and flung it to the ground.

Startled, the man jumped and dropped the book. Dark liquid splattered down the front of his shirt as his makeshift stool fell over, dumping him onto the ground. He stared up at her, his eyes big and round. "Wh-what did you say? Who *are* you?"

"I *said* this is my land! You are trespassing!"

A puzzled frown wrinkled a sunburned brow above the brightest blue eyes she had ever seen. He lay sprawled at her feet with his broad shoulders squeezed into a Garfield T-shirt, his dark hair in disarray—and covering most of his bronzed face.

He glanced down at himself, grinned and pushed nimbly to his feet.

Seeing how he towered over her, she backed off a step. Determined not to let him intimidate her, she quickly regained her stance and demanded, "Well! What do you have to say for yourself?"

He took his time brushing dust from his jeans and picking up the book from the ground. Then he looked at her. "I'm afraid you're mistaken, miss," he drawled. "This is my land. It is *you* who are trespassing."

His land! What did he mean, *his land?* Kate's knees began to buckle. The man's face swam before her eyes.

"Are you all right, miss?" He stuck the book under one arm and righted the makeshift stool. "Here. You'd best sit down. You don't look very good."

"Thanks. Most folks don't tell me so bluntly."

He threw back his head and laughed a deep hearty laugh that crinkled his eyes and exposed even white teeth above his dark beard. "I see you have a temper to go with the red hair. You must be the younger daughter. Your hair looks like your mother's and sister's."

"How do you know my mother and sister?"

"Met them when I bought the place." With one deft movement, he swept his shirts and cutoffs from the tree limb and rolled them into a ball.

"They *sold* the land to you?" She dropped to the log stool.

He pitched the ball of clothing inside the opening of a small tent and then turned to study her. "Joyce Sanderson—your mother?—and her brothers, Robert and Sidney Cummins, sold it to me."

Kate suddenly felt weak again, but she fought to keep him from seeing it. Still, she couldn't hide the fear in her voice as she asked, "What about the house?"

"The house?"

Her head jerked back. If he didn't know about the house, perhaps there was yet hope. "Over the hill there." She indicated the direction with her head.

"Oh. The old tumbled-down farmhouse."

"Tumbled *down!* It can't be!"

He stood another piece of firewood on end and sat down facing her. "It's not completely. But it would take too much work and money to make it livable again. And, yes, it belongs to me, too."

"They *couldn't* have sold it all to you. The house and this little strip of woods are mine. Grandpa said they would be."

"Perhaps he thought you'd inherit them from your mother."

"No. He knew he couldn't count on that."

"Were you planning to live here? Did you have some kind of special plans for the place?"

Her strength suddenly returned. She jumped up from the log. "*Was* I planning to live here? *Did* I have special plans? There's no past tense about it. I *will* get my land back. And I *will* live in my house again."

Turning on her heel, she stalked away from him. When she reached the edge of the clearing she heard him call, "You're welcome to walk in the woods anytime."

Without a backward glance she plunged into the trees.

When she was well out of the man's sight, she stopped and dropped to the ground under a giant oak tree. She needed time to calm down and think before she went back to the house. She didn't relish another scene with her mother.

Glancing at the stain on her shirt, she thought about the many times her mother had said to her, *I don't see why you can't be more like your sister and cousins, instead of running around with broken nails from playing in the dirt.*

Playing in the dirt. Cutting words meant to express her disapproval of Kate's chosen profession, horticulture, which she studied while working at a garden center near Auburn University. Rather, it *had been* her chosen career. This news may have put an end to her dream.

She leaned her head back against the tree trunk and stretched her long legs in front of her. She dashed a tear from her cheek. *I can't be like them, no matter how much Mother tries to make me. I can't be who I'm not, just to please her.*

But who am I anyway? What am I going to do with my life if the land really does belong to him?

Unbidden, words from a familiar verse of scripture came

to mind: *I know the plans I have for you, says the Lord, plans to give you hope and a future.*

Future? What kind of future? As for hope—

A bright orange-and-gold leaf drifted down beside her, lightly touching her cheek.

She looked up into the branches of trees high above her. Filtered sunlight glistened through the glorious autumn leaves. For the first time, she noticed the songs of birds filling the air.

A sudden flash of gray among the leaves caught her eyes. A squirrel skimmed along a branch of the oak. It paused at the end of the limb and then sailed through the air and landed on the branch of a tall pine. Darting from branch to swaying branch, it moved higher and higher until she could no longer see it.

She felt a faint smile touch her lips. The forest always had a way of making her feel at peace. And it felt so good to be back.

But now her mother had sold her land to a stranger. An infuriating, arrogant stranger. With a foolish grin and startling blue eyes.

This is my land. It is you who are trespassing.

She jumped to her feet and brushed at the seat of her jeans as she thought about his words. "We'll just see about that, Mr. High and Mighty. I'm going to get this land back. And I'm going to live in my house again."

She shot a menacing glance behind her, in the direction of a faint smell of wood smoke. Then she set out in a determined stride toward the house on the far side of the field.

It was about time she and her mother had an honest little talk.

In the woods behind her, Steve Adams stood staring at the opening in the trees, scratching his bearded chin. Was what she said true? Did the redheaded whirlwind actually have some kind of claim on the property?

If she does have a legal claim as one of the old man's heirs, she can hold up our operation indefinitely. He would wait and try to find out a little more about the woman before talking to the others about it.

He grinned thinking about her—the way she looked as he had stared up at her from where he lay on the ground. Her hands planted firmly on her hips, hair falling about her face, flaming red and gold in a streak of sunlight.

Getting to know her might be interesting—and fun—if the matter weren't so serious.

Frowning, he turned back to his campsite and looked across at the hillock where the first building would stand. He was almost ready to begin laying it out, driving in stakes and stringing up line. He'd already bought the materials, had them piled behind the old house, ready to haul over as soon as he widened the path enough to get his pickup through.

His frown deepened as he thought of the girl's words about the house. She was planning to live *there?* When she'd mentioned a house, he'd thought there surely must be a better building that he didn't know about someplace on the property.

He shook his head, trying to remove some of the cobwebs, and then glanced down at his coffee mug still lying on the ground. He grinned again, shaking his head in disbelief. Man, she was something else, the way she'd shot through those bushes at him. Likely to have scared him half to death. He would have thought a bear had him—if he'd had time to think anything.

Picking up the mug, he went to check for more coffee in the blackened pot on a rock near the remains of his fire.

A little later that evening, Kate stepped from her uncle's car onto the graveled parking lot of the small rural church her family had attended for four generations. Closing the car door, she glanced at the hillside behind the church building. White marble glistened in the setting sun. Several generations of her family lay out there under those markers. How she wished her grandfather could tell her what he had meant when he'd said one day his house and woods would belong to her.

"I'm glad you'll be with us awhile, Kate." Her aunt flashed her a smile as they walked toward the church house steps.

"Thanks, Aunt El. I appreciate your inviting me."

"With Charlotte off on the mission field and your uncle Rob on the road so much, it can get quite lonesome around our place at times."

"Yes, I'm glad you'll be there with Ellendor," her uncle agreed as they hurried up the steps.

They heard singing before they stepped onto the small porch. Kate frowned. "I'm sorry. I stayed in the woods so late I caused you to be late for church."

Her aunt glanced at her as her husband stepped around them to open the door. "I'm just glad you're here for the special Thanksgiving service. I think you'll like our new pastor. And you'll get to see a lot of folks you haven't seen in a long time."

Kate grimaced as she followed her aunt inside the building. *Seeing a lot of folks* was one of the last things she wanted to do. But she felt she couldn't refuse to attend the service after Aunt El and Uncle Rob had invited her to spend her Thanksgiving holiday with them.

"To thy house, Oh, Lord, with rejoicing we come, for we know that we are Thine…"

The familiar hymn reverberated through the old wooden structure where Kate had spent many happy hours of her childhood. She slid into a pew beside Aunt El and picked up a hymnal.

She couldn't help but smile at the feel of the familiar old book in her hand. It was good to see somebody still used hymnals.

She liked the praise songs churches were singing nowadays, the few churches she had visited during the past year or two, anyway. But it was good to be able to sing these familiar words again—and hold the worn book in her hands as she sang. It brought back happy memories of earlier times.

Times when she'd played barefoot around the farmhouse, gathered tomatoes from the garden, ran barefoot through the woods—

Her mother and her brothers had sold it to him.

Kate glanced at her aunt and uncle. Had there been a formal reading of Grandpa's will? If so, why had she not been told about it?

She was glad her parents had left for home while she was in the woods so she couldn't talk to her mother about the land as she'd meant to. She wasn't sure she could trust her mother about it. Who could she trust? Certainly not her sister, who was probably the attorney for the sale.

Maybe she'd find a lawyer for herself, have him check out the legitimacy of the sale and what rights she might have to part of the land.

"Be thankful and be glad!"

The words rang through the sanctuary as the preacher stepped into the pulpit, jarring Kate back to her surroundings.

"The Bible tells us God has wonderful plans for our lives here on this earth. Plans to give us a future and a hope. And Jesus Himself said He is preparing a wonderful place for us after this life is over. He has gone back to Heaven to prepare a home there just for you."

Oh, yeah? If He has, Mother will probably find a way to take mine over and sell it.

Kate's cheeks warmed at the irreverence of her thoughts. She turned her eyes from the minister's probing gaze to a window on the far side of the sanctuary and the marble stones barely visible in the evening light. She closed her eyes trying to envision this wonderful place the pastor described instead of the cold, dark graves out there.

Could she trust God to provide such a place when she died? Could she trust God to provide anything at all for her, here in this life or anyplace else, when He let all the things she loved most be taken away from her?

Biting back threatening tears, she ignored the minister's words as she stared out the window at the gathering darkness.

Soon, the white tombstones and bright flowers at the grave sites were no longer visible.

Like her future, only a black void remained.

Chapter 2

A pregnant young woman in a white top and black pants ushered Kate into the inner office. The man behind the massive desk stood and extended a hand. He was almost as tall as the man camping in her woods, but there was no comparison in their appearances.

L. Paul Boyer, attorney-at-law, looked a few years older than the man who had taken over her land. He looked forty, at least. He had a slender build instead of broad shoulders. He sported what was obviously a salon-styled haircut, short with sides and the top brushed up neatly from a clean-shaven face. His clothing was in sharp contrast to the intruder's. Instead of a silly T-shirt and rough woodsmen's boots, he wore a dark suit with a snowy-white dress shirt and red tie.

Conscious of her own untidiness, Kate wiped her sweaty hands down the sides of her jeans before shaking hands with him. Her cheeks grew hot as his smooth hand with immaculate nails enveloped her work-roughened hand with its stained, uneven nails.

"Have a seat, Miss Sanderson." He resumed his seat behind the desk.

Kate tugged at the hem of her blue T-shirt and sat on the edge of the padded chair across from him. She curled her hands in her lap to hide her nails.

"Now, Miss Sanderson, tell me what you wish to talk to me about." His voice was as smooth as his appearance.

"Well, I—" She took a deep breath, and her next words came out in a rush. "Someone is trying to take my land."

He nodded. "Yes. Go on."

"He says he bought it, but it's rightfully mine." She hadn't intended to sound so defiant, but the mere thought of the arrogant man in the woods irritated her.

The attorney settled back in his big leather chair. "Suppose you tell me the whole story, then we'll see if I might help you."

His calmness helped calm Kate a bit. She slid back in the chair.

"When my grandfather died, he left some land. He had already given land to his children to build homes—but my mother sold hers and moved away. I didn't expect all that was left to be mine, but he knew how I loved the place. I was with him a lot before I went off to school, took care of him after his tractor accident and first stroke. I found him after the big one and—"

She realized she was babbling and stopped.

The man cleared his throat. "Tell me about the property you expected to have. Have you talked with your mother about the sale?"

"No!" Kate slid forward to the edge of the chair. "And I don't want her to know I talked with you about it. If she knew, she'd find some way to block anything I might be able to do, especially since her daughter—my older sister—is a lawyer."

His brows went up, and then he nodded. "I assure you, Miss Sanderson, whatever you tell me will be held in strictest confidence."

"Thank you." She settled back in the chair.

"And who is this person who claims to have bought the property?"

"I…don't know his name. I only met him— Well, saw him briefly yesterday in the woods. Can you find out some way?"

"Possibly." He picked up a pen and held it poised over a note pad. "When did he allegedly purchase it?"

"I don't know. Grandpa died less than two months ago."

"Was there a will?"

"If there was one, nobody said anything to me about it." *How surprising is that?*

The lawyer cleared his throat. "I see." He picked up the pen again. "All right, I'll see what I can do and—"

The phone on his desk buzzed. "Excuse me." He picked up the receiver. "Yes, Jane?"

After a brief pause, he added, "Put her on."

Looking at Kate, he said, "I'll only be a minute. If you'll excuse me—" He swung his chair round with his back to her. "Hello, Claire. How was the flight?"

The crackle of a feminine voice vibrated over the line.

He sighed. "Yes. Of course. I'll work it out. Again. I'll have Mrs. Mason stay over with the kids."

Kate turned to stare out the window at the traffic passing on Main Street. But she could still hear his end of the conversation.

"Lisa cried last night because she misses you." His voice was heavy with irritation. "Most people want to spend Thanksgiving with their families, you know."

He lowered his voice. "I *know* she's almost a teenager. That doesn't stop her from missing her mother."

Kate stood and turned toward the door. That was all she needed, a lawyer with domestic issues. He had enough of his own problems without taking on hers.

"Claire, I have to go.

"Miss Sanderson?" He hung up the phone.

Kate looked at him.

"You can give Jane the names of the people involved, and your phone number, and I'll see what I can do. Jane will call you to set up an appointment when I have something."

Driving toward her aunt's house, Kate found herself humming one of the more lively tunes from yesterday's church service. If Mr. Boyer could get things straightened out by the time school let out for Christmas holidays, she would come back here until winter session.

She smiled, thinking about the old house, the way it stood white in the sun, its long front porch shaded by sweet-smelling wisteria and honeysuckle in spring and summer, and rain playing softly on the tin roof in fall and winter. She could almost smell the burning logs in the rock fireplace.

Burning logs. Her mind flew to the man from the woods.

Grrrrind. A sudden lurch and grinding noise jerked her thoughts back to the present. Slamming on the brakes, she felt the little car tilt sideways. "I can't believe this! Why did I try something so foolish?"

Unmindful, she had turned onto the rutted driveway leading to the old house. She put on the emergency brake and pounded the steering wheel with her fist.

Crawling out of the car, she stooped and peered underneath. No major dents or scrapes. Not yet anyway. Maybe she could put the car in Reverse and back up the hill.

But it would not move backward any more than forward. Transferring her foot from the accelerator to the brake pedal, she laid her aching head against the steering wheel and groaned aloud. "This is just what I needed."

Well, sitting there fuming was not going to solve anything. She crawled out of the car and stared at the two tires sitting in a rut. She might be able to pile brush under the tires and give them some traction.

She stood and glanced around for fallen limbs and sticks.

Behind the house, at the edge of the yard, a perspiring Steve Adams hacked away at bushes and vines blocking a trail through the woods. He stopped to wipe sweat from his eyes with the sleeve of his denim shirt. Whew, it was awfully warm for late November.

He didn't mind the heat so much, if the rain would just hold off so he could get some work done.

Picking up a small insulated jug from the ground, he turned it up to drink from the spout, and stopped. Was something bumping down the washed-out driveway?

He cocked his head to one side and listened. A picture of the young woman who had challenged him in the woods flashed into his mind. He couldn't help smiling as he recalled the way she had stood glaring down at him as he lay on the ground stunned by her sudden, almost violent appearance in the peaceful woodland setting.

But he knew the situation was no laughing matter—for him or for her. He wouldn't be at all surprised if she did decide to check out the old house.

He listened again, but the bumping had stopped. More than likely a train in the distance. Turning up the jug, he drank long and deep, then set it down. He picked up the machete and began swinging it again.

After a few minutes, he stopped hacking and glanced down the trail he had cleared from his camping spot to the backyard of the old farmhouse. He would widen it more later so trucks could get through.

He headed back to the old house again, planning to go inside this time and look around, see if there was anything he could salvage.

The back steps appeared too rotten to hold his weight, so he made his way round to the front. The steps there didn't look much sturdier, but he approached them cautiously and crossed the rickety porch to the front door. Something inside the door prevented him from opening it enough to go inside, so he leaned over, put his eye to the crack and peered in.

Part of a large tree limb had fallen through the roof and was blocking the doorway. He'd go back to camp and get his power saw and see if he could cut his way inside.

He moved back across the porch and down the steps. At the corner of the house, he paused and glanced in the direction of the pitted roadway leading from the main road. A funny scratching sound came from up the hill. Surely that crazy redhead wouldn't try to drive over all those ruts and boulders.

It was probably a county work crew filling in potholes on the main road. He made a mental note to work on the driveway in the near future—before someone, like that stubborn woman, did try to drive down it in a low-slung automobile.

He listened again to the scratching. *Don't know why I keep watching for her to reappear.* It wasn't as if he believed she really had a legitimate claim on the land.

Still, he couldn't get her off his mind. Maybe it was because he felt sorry for her losing her grandfather and then learning he had not left her his home as he had promised.

Well, it wasn't his problem. He'd bought the place in good faith. And he had a lot of work to do on it before winter set in. Right now, he'd better get his mind off her and retrieve the saw. He glanced again in the direction of the roadway and then set out in a lope across the overgrown yard toward the woodland trail.

On the washed-out roadway leading to the farmhouse, Kate wiped her perspiring forehead with the back of her arm. She surveyed the pile of twigs and small rocks she had packed into a rut in front of the Escort. Hopefully, these would prevent the tires from sinking deeper in the hole. She climbed into the driver's seat, started the engine and began to inch forward.

Whew! She made it through that one. Now, if she could get around the ditch that loomed up ahead.

Fighting to avoid the deeper ruts and larger stones, her mind was completely absorbed in trying to keep the car— and herself—from real harm. When she finally slid around the last curve, her foot involuntarily jammed on the brakes. Her head almost hit the windshield.

"How could they? How could they let it go to ruin this way?"

It seemed impossible the place could have gone down so quickly from disuse. Had it begun deteriorating even before she'd left for college, and she had been too preoccupied to notice?

She stared in disbelief at the beloved house. Overgrown weeds and shrubs covered the windows. Vines crept up the walls and rock chimney. A fallen limb jutted from a hole in the roof.

"I can't believe it. I just can't believe it."

She dashed a tear from her cheek and turned off the car. She made her way through the tangle of weeds and vines in the yard and up the crumbling steps, across broken and sagging boards of the porch. But something inside prevented her from opening the door.

She put an eye against the crack and peeped in. The inside was almost as bad as the outside.

Several windowpanes were broken. The sofa was saggy and covered in dust and grime. Once-pretty bright red curtains now hung in faded tatters. Wallpaper was peeling from the walls in places.

She repositioned her eye at the crack so she could see the corner where the desk sat. This was where she'd found her grandfather after his first stroke.

He had appeared to be fine before the stroke hit him. He'd had an enjoyable three-day visit with two old army buddies. They'd had breakfast at McDonald's, lunch at the new buffet place in town. They'd played dominoes, pulled out pictures from army days and talked about old times. The men had left only the day before the stroke.

Grandpa had seemed a little tired when Kate left for school that morning, but she thought it was only from all the activity of the past few days. He told her not to worry about him; he was fine, going to spend the day resting and catching up on paperwork. He'd asked her if she could drive him to town after school that afternoon so he could run some errands.

But when she'd gotten home she'd found him on the floor beside the desk.

Peering through the crack in the door, she relived the scene.

He'd lain very still, eyes closed, writing pen clutched in his hand. Papers from the desk surrounded him on the floor. When she'd rushed to him and placed her hand on his forehead, he'd opened his eyes and tried to speak. But his mouth was twisted in an odd way and spittle dribbled into his gray beard. When his words came out garbled, she knew it was more than just a fall.

Hush, Grandpa, she'd whispered. *Be quiet now. Everything will be all right.*

She had jumped up, grabbed the telephone, dialed 911 and then called her uncle Rob.

Sitting on the floor beside her grandfather, she'd cradled his head in her lap. *I love you, Grandpa. You can't leave me.*

Lo-love you, Kate. He'd struggled to sit up. *Pa-papers—Desk.*

Yes, I see them. I'll mail the checks. Be still. Lie back down.

He'd struggled harder to sit. And to speak. *Pa-papers.*

I'll take care of the papers, Grandpa. Now hush. Rest. Tears had streamed down her face. *I'll take care of everything for you. And I'll take care of you. I promise.*

Remembering, tears streamed down her face now, too. "Mother didn't allow me to take care of everything for you the way I promised, Grandpa," she whispered, as though he were there to hear her. "But I did the best I could to take care of *you*."

She tore her gaze from the crack in the door and wiped her tears on the tail of her T-shirt. She stretched her neck and then stepped carefully across the rotted boards of the porch to the crumbling stone steps. She sat down on the top step and returned to the past.

Her grandfather had seemed too disoriented to understand her words of reassurance. He'd continued to ramble on about "papers," even as he was being loaded into the ambulance. So, before driving to the hospital, she'd quickly gathered up the checks and other papers scattered about the floor and stuffed them into her shoulder bag.

Sorting them later, she found a gas bill but no check to the gas company, and the checkbook was missing. When she didn't find them in the desk drawer or under the desk, she called her mother over at Uncle Rob's house.

"Yes," her mother snapped. "I found the checkbook on the floor, but I didn't find a check. You can give the gas bill to me. Don't you worry about Father's business affairs. It's not your place to take care of them. I'll be taking care of things from now on."

Her grandfather had never been able to speak clearly again. Off and on through the years he would try to talk to her about the "papers."

Kate had tried to explain that her mother had mailed all the checks, including a new one she'd written to the gas company. But he'd continued to bring it up, as if his mind was stuck in the unfinished task.

Straightening herself on the step, Kate took a deep breath and stood. Well, she couldn't sit there thinking about the past forever. She had to get on with the present. Maybe she could get inside through the back door, see if anything in there was still any good.

Tramping through the weeds to the end of the house, she rounded the corner—and stopped short. Her mouth dropped open, then snapped shut. She stared at the dark late-model pickup sitting in the backyard.

Weeds and briars were trampled down between the house and the path leading through the woods toward the stranger's camp. It appeared as though the trail was recently widened.

So, it's beyond repair, is it?

If he really thought the house was too far gone to use, why had he gone to the trouble of clearing a path to it? What had he been hauling to it—or away from it—in a pickup truck?

More than ever, she was sure something was shady about the sale of the place.

Maybe the man was bluffing about buying it. With that bushy beard and those ratty blue jeans, he looked as though he could be a fugitive from the law.

Sudden loud singing—or bellowing—came from the woods.

Her heart beating wildly, Kate jumped behind a bush at the corner of the house.

That man was striding up the trail through the trees,

swinging a machete in one hand and a power saw in the other, singing loud and off-key.

My, how he loved this place! Fresh air. Beautiful autumn colors. Freedom to sing as loud as he wished. With head thrown back, arms and shoulders keeping rhythm, he sang at the top of his lungs, "Everybody, come on, praise the Lord. Praise the Lord. Praise—"

A sudden movement beside the old house halted his singing and his movement. He stopped just outside the tree line and squinted in the bright sunlight as a blue shape darted around the corner of the house. When he heard a car start, he took off in a run toward the sound.

He reached the front porch in time to watch a small blue sedan chew its way up the old driveway. Through the rear window, he caught a glimpse of flowing red hair. Smiling, he shook his head. What in the world would she do next? His next thought surprised him: *I can't wait to find out.*

Chapter 3

Kate sat on a back doorstep staring at the woods across the garden patch. She took another nibble of her turkey sandwich.

"I'll get it back," she said to the fat brown wren watching from the bottom of the steps. "Some way, I'll get it back."

She tossed a pinch of the sandwich to the chirping bird and returned her gaze to the woods. What had the intruder cut with the saw he was carrying this morning? What did he plan to do with the place? How much would he fight to keep it?

Despite her musings about his evil intentions, he hadn't appeared much of a threat sprawled on the ground in that ridiculous Garfield T-shirt.

She smiled, thinking about it—until she recalled the way he towered over her when he stood.

"But he doesn't intimidate *me* with those broad shoulders and that condescending smile."

The bird cocked its head to one side and stared at her as if to say, *Sure he doesn't.*

"Well, he doesn't. And I won't run away from him again."

She tossed the remainder of the sandwich to the bird and jumped to her feet.

"'It is *you* who is trespassing. But you're welcome to walk in *my* woods,'" she muttered, mocking his words. "As though I need his permission to walk on my property."

She would walk where she'd always walked, whenever she pleased. She'd just keep away from him, not because she was afraid of him but because she couldn't stand the sight of him.

However, it was as though an unseen magnet drew her to his camp. Easing near an opening in the brush, she bent and peered between the leaves at his empty campsite.

"Aha! Do we have a spy here?"

Kate jumped and whirled round. And almost fell into the arms of the big, bearded stranger.

"I am not spying. I was…out walking—where I have every right to walk and…"

He grinned. "And decided to stop by my camp for a little visit." With a deep bow, he swept out an arm to grant her entry through the break in the trees and underbrush. "Welcome to my humble abode."

She hesitated only a moment before preceding him into the camp area. She'd hang around for a while and see if she could find out exactly what he was up to here in her woods.

He stood two of the short, fat logs on end. "Have a seat and make yourself comfortable while I pour us some tea."

Kate balanced herself on one of the makeshift stools and watched as the man poked his head inside his tiny tent and pulled out a couple of colorful mugs. After setting the mugs on a crudely built picnic table, he took a jug from an ice chest beside the tent, poured amber-colored liquid into each cup and handed her the red one.

He placed the jug back in the chest and turned to her. "Drink up," he said, raising his blue cup in salute.

Kate shot him a sour look and waited while he straddled a log stool and balanced his tall frame on it. Wrapping his long, brown fingers around his mug, he smiled at her.

Kate felt herself blush when she realized she had been checking for a wedding ring. He might have pulled it off while he worked.

But it was nothing to her one way or the other.

She ducked her head and took a sip of tea to calm the sensation in the pit of her stomach.

"A penny," he said, leaning toward her.

She jumped. "Huh?"

He chuckled. "A penny for your thoughts, as the old saying goes. Football? Boyfriend? School?" He stretched out his long, jeans-clad legs and leaned back against a tree.

"I don't like football. I don't have a boyfriend. And I'm not leaving here and going back to school as long as you're taking up residence on my land."

He studied her. "I think your mother told me you attend university? Your senior year?"

She narrowed her eyes. "What else did my mother tell you about me?"

"Why? Is there something she should have told me?"

He said it in a teasing way, but she didn't find the situation humorous. "Not unless it was to say I won't sit still while she sells our family's land out from under me!"

He arched an eyebrow, drained his cup and then looked at her again. "So, you're not a schoolgirl. Just a lady of leisure, then?"

She shrugged. "Actually, I'm not much of anything."

He crossed his arms over his denim-covered chest, his empty mug dangling from one finger. "Yes, I suppose we all feel that way at times. But we're really worth quite a lot. Have you ever thought about all the planning that went into bringing us into existence?"

"Planning? Huh. Someone may have planned for you. But my parents wanted a boy when I was born. They already had their perfect little girl."

He didn't bat an eye. "I'm not speaking of the plans our parents make. They really don't have much of a say in what we'll be when we're born. I'm thinking of something the Psalmist said."

"Yes, I know. 'You created my inmost being; you knit me together in my mother's womb. I am fearfully and wonderfully made.'"

Kate didn't mean to sound sarcastic quoting Scripture. But he was so…irritating!

"Beautiful, isn't it, knowing we were carefully designed. For instance, your red hair didn't just happen—nor did my big nose…."

"You don't have a big nose."

She felt her cheeks grow hot again. What made her say such a thing? It didn't matter to her whether he had a nice nose—which he had—or one as big as Texas. All she wanted was to get him off her land. And as quickly as possible.

He grinned, whether at her words or her pink cheeks, she didn't know. And really didn't care.

"'All the days ordained for me were written in your book before one of them came to be.'" He was quoting more Scripture at her. "God planned a wonderful life for each of us."

There was that Scripture staring her in the face, again.

She glanced around the clearing, then up at the bright leafy canopy spread above them. "I can see why *you* would think so. I used to believe the same thing. But it seems all my dreams—and my beautiful life—died when you showed up."

"God knows the plans He has for us, even when we don't. Plans to prosper us, to give us hope and a future."

He spoke gently, and that irritated her even more. "I know that verse, too. So, if you're preaching at me, please don't."

Her thoughts from this morning, about him being a member of a blood-sacrificing cult, flitted through her mind. But she dismissed them. He was more likely some overly zealous religious nut. "Who are you anyway?"

A smile lit his eyes and tugged at the corners of his mouth. He reached up and smoothed the dark growth below his finely shaped lips, then touched the ax propped against the tree beside him. "Me? Why, I'm just a lonely wood-chopper, ma'am, craving a little conversation—and maybe a drop of human kindness?"

Kate hopped to her feet, overturning her makeshift stool. "Well, don't expect kindness from me. And you had best stop chopping trees until you find out whose land you're chopping on."

Her words wiped the smile from his face. "Would you care to walk the land lines with me and show me where *your* property lies?"

He stood as though ready to begin stepping off boundaries.

"No, I—" Flustered, she realized she didn't know exactly where any of the property lines were. All of her life, she had been free to roam wherever she pleased in the wooded area belonging to her family and their neighbors.

"You can show me the ground you were supposed to have, and I can show you what we purchased from your family and Mr. Atkins."

"You bought land from Mr. Atkins, too?" What was the man planning to do with so much land?

"The old fields over there." He nodded toward the west. "That's where we'll have gardens and barns for the horses."

"Horses? *We* will have gardens and horses? Who is *we?*"

He studied her as she glared at him. The golden specks in her eyes sparkled. Evidently she had not spoken to anyone about him since yesterday. It was obvious no one had told her anything about the land deal.

"I'm sorry, I should have introduced myself."

She whirled away from him, crossing her arms as though warding off his answer. "It doesn't matter to me in the least who you are. You won't be around here much longer."

He could tell by her stance that she was waiting for him to tell her anyway.

But he didn't. He could be just as stubborn as she. "Look, do you have time to walk over the property with me?" He smiled at her.

She turned back to him, subdued. "It's beginning to look as though time may be all I do have—now."

He discarded the smile. "Shall we go for that walk, then?"

She shrugged. "Sure. Why not?"

He smiled. She was likely thinking she'd stick around long enough to discover what he was doing here and how she might find a way to claim the place. And what harm would it do to let her try?

Meantime, he'd learn more about her, what she was thinking and what she was likely to attempt.

She walked silently behind him along a narrow trail beaten through the trees by rabbits, deer and dogs. The forest was quiet; the only sound was the crunch of their shoes on dry leaves.

When they reached an area where hardwood trees and heavy underbrush gave way to pines, he dropped back to walk beside her. Their shoes made soft, squeaky sounds on the thick layer of pine needles, sending up a pleasing, pungent aroma as it crushed beneath their feet.

Still neither of them spoke.

He touched her arm lightly. She didn't protest but stopped as he pointed at a spot on the straw-covered ground just ahead of them.

A gray squirrel sat on his haunches gnawing contentedly on a pine cone, seemingly unaware of the humans standing motionless only a few feet from him. But when a second squirrel ran down the trunk of a nearby tree, the first ceased chewing and dropped the cone to chase the intruder away. Like she wanted to do.

The squirrels ran up a tall pine. Branches dipped and swayed as one chased the other down one limb and then another. Then the tiny feet of the pursuer slipped on a limb. Hanging by only his forefeet, he swung underneath until he could regain his footing.

Kate watched with him, laughing softly, before they began walking again.

"They come into camp and play like that sometimes. Here, this way." He took her elbow to steer her onto an old logging road.

When Kate glanced at him he didn't drop his hand. Her lips tightened, but she didn't pull away.

Birds darted about overhead and in and out of trees on each side of them as they walked. Other small creatures, startled by the noise of their footsteps, scurried through the leaves at the edge of the track and into the undergrowth. A break in the trees made by the old road bed let in sunlight and warmed their shoulders and backs. They simultaneously slowed their pace, letting the sun beat down on them.

As they rounded a bend, the roadway narrowed to a path between towering pines, ancient oaks and hickory trees.

Limbs overlapped above the path, blocking out most of the sunlight and creating a tunnel effect.

"Reminds you of a great cathedral, doesn't it?" he asked in hushed tones. Kate nodded, and after a moment they began silently walking again.

Moving beneath the canopy of trees, her spirit was oddly in agreement with his. The beauty of the forest was weaving peace about him, too.

A loud chirping broke through her reverie and she glanced up, searching for its source. If a casual observer heard it without seeing the small creature, he might think the sound only the twitter of a bird. But Kate recognized it at once.

"It's a big bird up there someplace." He glanced up at the tree limb over their heads and stopped.

"No." She stopped with him and pointed into the branches. "It's a squirrel. I've heard them enough to know. See..." The small gray-and-white creature sat on a limb near the trunk of the tree, watching them down below.

He smiled down at her. "You're a real woodland nymph, aren't you?"

She gave him a wry smile and continued walking. He followed.

As they emerged from the trees, he pointed at a small rocky knoll off the beaten path. "Let's go up over that hill. We can see out across the pastureland from there."

She tensed and glared at him.

"I'm telling you something you already know, aren't I?"

Her demeanor changed from hostile to sadness. "When I was a child, that area was covered in trees, too. The Johnson family owned it. Their ancestors settled it."

"As your ancestors settled this land?"

"Yes. Doesn't *your* family own land someplace?"

Her anger was back. Maybe he should let her get used to things a little at a time. "Not anymore. Interstates took it. It was just outside Atlanta. My dad's a retired minister. He and Mom bought another house, but need more room. They take care of several homeless boys."

"Is there not room for just one more?"

He frowned. "One more?"

"You. Isn't there room for you among the other homeless boys?"

He couldn't help laughing. A sharp wit and a sharp tongue. "Actually, a housing development is taking it."

"So you come here to take mine."

Refusing to get into another argument, he turned from her and pushed aside the limbs of a prickly bush for her to pass. He took her elbow to help guide her through the briars and brush.

Kate knocked his hand away and trudged up the rocky hill in front of him, making her way around briars and boulders. When she slipped, he reached out to steady her but quickly took his hand away. Regaining her footing, she marched onward.

A lone tree stood at the top of the hill. A shortleaf pine. When they reached it, they dropped down below its spindly branches. As their weight crushed sun-warmed pine needles, its warm tangy aroma rose to greet their nostrils.

He sighed and stretched out on his back, resting his head on interlaced fingers. His dark hair, damp and curling from the heat of exertion, brushed lightly against her arm, and something squeezed within her stomach. She caught a deep breath and moved slightly away from him.

He gazed up at the sky and asked lazily, "See that stallion up there?"

"Stallion? Where?"

"Right up there." He pointed at a bank of cumulus clouds. "Next to the lady in the ballroom gown."

Kate laughed despite herself. "My cousin Charlotte and I used to pick out shapes in the clouds when we were kids."

"Well, let's see how good you are at it now. See if you can find a canoe and a—a canoe with a dog—no! It's an elephant. A canoe with an elephant in it. Come on! Quick! Before it changes."

She laughed again and stretched out on her back on the bed of soft pine needles. But not close enough to touch him.

Gazing upward, her eyes picked out the cloud she thought he was referring to. "Right there!" She pointed, jubilant. "Just to the right of that—that *pig*."

"Pig? I don't see a pig. Yes, I guess that could be a pig. And look! One leg just floated away."

They laughed together.

"Okay. Let's see a—" He squinted, concentrating on the sky. "Let's see you find a—a porpoise jumping for a minnow. Come on! Quick." He turned to her, laughter in his voice. "It's beginning to—" His voice trailed off. She felt him studying her.

She didn't answer. The fun had suddenly gone out of the game.

"What have you found?" He spoke softly. He didn't want to send her off into another one of her quicksilver, angry moods. But he didn't want her going catatonic on him, either. "What do you see up there now?"

"Ink spots!" She pushed herself to a sitting position and turned on him. "You sound like a shrink. 'Look at the pretty spots, Katerina. What do you see in this one? How about that one over there?'"

In one swift movement she jumped to her feet and went running back down the hill in the direction from which they had come. Just before he caught up to her, her foot slid across a stone and she fell sprawling, facedown.

He squatted beside her and reached out a hand to touch her shoulder. "Are you all right? Are you hurt?"

"Go away and leave me alone." She buried her face in her arms.

He rocked back on his heels and waited for her to calm down. After a minute, when she kept lying there, he touched her shoulder. "Will you at least let me help you up?"

"No."

"If you're not hurt, get up and let's go."

She raised a tear-streaked face. "Just go away."

"It's not that simple. Nothing in real life is, you know." He didn't mean to sound so harsh. He softened his tone. "Here, let me help you up."

"No! Don't touch me. I can get up by myself."

He stood and watched as she slowly lifted herself to her feet and began brushing at her jeans. When she winced, he reached out and took both her hands in his. She tried to pull away, as he knew she would, but he turned her palms up to examine them.

"You have some pretty nasty scratches here. They need to be cleaned. I have some antiseptic back at camp. How about the rest of you? Feel like anything is broken?"

"No." She stood still while he brushed the tangle of hair from her face.

He was surprised she was so submissive. Probably not accustomed to having someone show this kind of concern for her, to look after her. From their brief conversation the other day, it sounded as though she'd always been the one to do the looking after.

He gently touched her forehead. "You have a slight cut here. Probably from a stone. Let's head back to camp so we can take care of it."

This time, when he took her arm, she did not object.

But when she tried to walk, she winced and pulled her arm from his grasp. Bending forward, she lifted the right leg of her jeans.

"Here, let me look at that." He stooped to examine her scraped knee.

"It's only a scratch. It's not the first time."

"I'm sure it's not. I'll roll up the hem so it won't rub against your knee as you walk."

"I'll do it."

He waited for her to turn the rough denim up to just above her injured knee. Then he took her arm again.

They walked slowly, and she limped only slightly.

"Does it hurt much?"

"No. I'm all right." She sounded embarrassed and refused to look at him.

They walked a few paces more.

"Katerina, huh? It's a very pretty name."

"Yeah." She still didn't look at him. "Sounds like a name for someone graceful, doesn't it? Like a ballerina, maybe. Boy, have my folks been disappointed. Most people call me Kate. Fits a klutz better."

"You're too hard on yourself."

She tried to shrug, but his hold on her arm prevented it. "You don't have to hold on to me!"

But when he let go of her arm, she looked disappointed. He suppressed a smile.

After they'd slowly covered a few more feet, he suggested, "Why don't you sit down on that fallen tree over there? I'll go bring the pickup around."

"No. I can walk fine. There's a spring through those trees." She nodded at a stand of trees just ahead of them. "I can wash off the dirt in it."

"A spring?" He'd never noticed a spring. "I've seen some wet, swampy spots, but no spring."

She didn't reply or wait for him, but struck out through the trees, hobbling on her injured leg.

He hurried after her. She stopped near a thick row of low bushes. "Do you hear it?"

He cocked an ear to listen and heard a faint trickle of water. "You can't get through all that brush to the water, especially with an injured knee."

"I know. It needs to be cut. Besides, there's a low bank on the other side." She hobbled to the edge of the line of bushes and tried to peep over, wobbling on the underbrush.

He hurried up and grasped her arm. "Be careful, you'll fall. Let me look." He bent as far as he could over the brush. "All I see is a bed of wet, flat rocks with one little trickle of water that's clogged with bushes and debris."

"The water comes from a spring in the rocks."

"Yeah. It needs a lot of cleaning." He raised up and looked at her. "Let's go back to camp. I have a first-aid box there. Do you want me to bring the pickup round for you?"

"No." Supporting herself with a stick, she hobbled alongside him back to camp.

He poured water from a plastic jug into a pan for her to wash her face and hands.

After she finished, he handed her a towel. "If you'll sit on this log over here, I'll help you clean the scrapes on your head and knee."

When the alcohol-soaked gauze touched the cut on Kate's knee, she bit her lip to keep from crying out.

He winced, too. "Sorry. Sometimes we have to hurt to heal."

She darted a look at his face. What did he mean by that remark?

He concentrated on cleaning the wounds on her head, hands and knee. Then he gently applied antiseptic cream to them and put a loose bandage over the scrape on her knee. When he finished, he stepped back and admired his handiwork. "You'll soon be good as new."

Two rows of even white teeth glistened through the black beard.

Feeling a funny tingle in her stomach, she jerked her gaze from his face and began rolling down her jean leg.

"Okay?" he asked when she stood to test the injured leg.

"Better, thanks. I need to get going."

"Let me find you something to drink first. It's still surprisingly hot out here and you've got to be thirsty after that trek we made."

Taking a glass jug filled with clear liquid from the cooler, he removed the lid and turned it up to pour some into the red mug she'd drunk from earlier.

"What is it?"

"Water. Clear, kind-of-cool, hauled-from-the-gas-station tap water. But now, thanks to my new neighbor, I can soon have fresh spring water."

He finished pouring into the red mug and then filled his blue one.

"You and I *are* neighbors, aren't we?" He handed her the red mug. "Temporarily, anyway."

She cast him a hostile glare over the rim of the mug. "*Temporary* is right. For you anyhow." She turned up the mug and drained it, then stood. "I'll be back."

"You'll come back soon and help me clean out the spring?"

"I knew there was some reason you were being so nice to me." She thrust the empty mug at him.

"I only thought you might like nice, cool spring water next time instead of this tepid, watered-down chlorine."

"Next time? What makes you think there will be a next time—with you anyhow? Maybe I'll clean out the spring alone and…" she glanced around his camp "…and stay here alone—after I get my land back."

"Until then, why can't we work on the spring *together?*"

She shot him a defiant look. Why not? If he wanted to help clean out her spring, she'd take advantage of the manpower.

"Okay. When do we start?" She glared at him defiantly, but when she caught his eye, she saw him smiling warmly. What was his angle? She wasn't going to stop until she'd figured him out.

Chapter 4

"Let's call it a morning and go have lunch."

Kate glanced at him and nodded…and kept raking.

He shook wet leaves and pine straw from his rake and leaned it against a tree.

A giggle escaped Kate's lips.

"What?"

"You have mud in your beard."

He grinned and wiped at it with a muddy hand, plastering more slime from the spring into the scraggly whiskers.

Laughing, she laid down the rake, stepped toward him and lifted a hand toward his face. When he leaned toward her and stuck out his chin, she realized what she was about to do and withdrew her hand.

He grinned and pulled in his chin. "You like cold grilled chicken?"

"Sure." She picked up a rock and moved it.

He bent, scooped water from the muddy stream and patted it into his beard. "Better?"

Kate smiled. "Not much."

Walking beside him back to camp, she thought about how well they had worked together that morning, although their only conversation had been what was necessary for the job.

When they sat down at the weathered picnic table to eat, he reached for her hand and bowed his head. Listening to him pray, she found it difficult to reconcile in her mind this congenial, gentle man with the scheming enemy she had described to the lawyer. But she wouldn't let him deter her from her goal.

When he released her hand, her fingers tingled from his touch.

"Dig in," he said. "It's simple, but filling."

Tired and hungry, though relaxed from the physical exercise, they talked little as they devoured his cold chicken, canned beans and grapes. Afterward, he picked up his cup and moved from the table to sit on the ground with his back against a tree. He stretched out his long legs and crossed them.

Revived by the food, Kate stood and began clearing the table.

"What's your rush?" He sounded sleepy. "Let's rest a bit before we clean up."

He watched her from beneath heavy eyelids.

Feeling a funny tingling in her stomach, she turned away. "I'm not tired."

She didn't want to sit around and socialize, giving him more opportunity to try to win her over with his wide, white smile and those blue eyes that crinkled at the corners when he laughed. She shot him a hostile glare. "Are you going to work some more, or sit here all day?"

He chuckled. "Slave-driving woman if I ever saw one."

She ignored his remark as she started for the spring.

* * *

He stood and set his cup on the table. She was an interesting woman, if he'd ever seen one. He grinned to himself as he followed her back to the spring.

He never knew what to expect when she opened her mouth to speak, or when he looked at her eyes. One moment she was berating herself, the next him, while the golden speckles in her green eyes sparked like flames of fire. Or she might lapse into a moody silence as her eyes turned dark, almost brown.

And he couldn't tell what action she might take concerning the property that she insinuated he and her mother had stolen from her. She vacillated between a fierce determination to fight for the land and a passive acceptance of its loss along with the loss of all her hopes and plans.

He had never before found it so difficult to read a woman. Or any person, for that matter. He'd always felt, and been told, that one of his God-given talents was his insight into people. This was one of the things that made him so good at his work. But this woman…

He smiled and shook his head as he watched her pick up a rake and step toward the spring.

Kate looked up from her raking and watched as he bent to pick up a large stone. Maybe she should act a little more agreeable, see how much work she could get out of him before Mr. Boyer found a way for her to put him off the land.

She smiled when he raised up and looked at her. "It used to be deep enough just below this for me to swim in."

At his look of surprise, she laughed, a real laugh, not a put-on. "Well, not deep enough to really swim. But I thought I was swimming. It was here I learned to hold my breath under water and kick and flap my arms. Even in the middle of summer, it was *so* cold. On a hot, sticky day, it felt really good to splash around in it."

He reached up to swipe the perspiration from his face with the tail of his denim shirt. Eyeing the shallow stream, then her, he grinned. "Do we dare?"

"No, it's about to get cold. Nights are already pretty cool."

"But it's hot today. Unseasonably so. Maybe we could just wet our feet? And dash a little on our faces?"

She glanced at the spring, caught her bottom lip between her teeth and looked at him.

Unable to resist the mock pleading in his eyes, she smiled.

Grinning at each other like mischievous children, they put aside tools and began untying muddy sneakers.

"You have to step in all at once," she warned as he stepped gingerly toward the stream in bare feet and jeans rolled to the knees. "If you don't, you'll back out."

He was dipping a bare toe in the chilly water when she reached out playfully to push him.

She let out a loud yell as she went down. Realizing too late he had sidestepped her touch, she fell on hands and knees into the chilly water.

The sudden shock of it took her breath away. Then she let out another loud yelp.

Laughing, he bent to help her up. She came up laughing but shivering. Her jeans legs were wet and her shirt splattered with muddy water.

"You'll catch your death of cold," he said, and gathered her close to warm her.

Nestled in his arms, she no longer felt cold. But she shivered even harder.

"We'd better get back to camp and dry you out," he said softly.

With his arm still around her, she shivered as he led her back.

At his campsite he grabbed a blanket from inside the tent

and wrapped it around her. She sat on a log and huddled inside the blanket watching as he built a fire. Whoever he was, whatever he did, he was not afraid of manual labor. But he talked like an educated man.

He turned from the fire and smiled. "Do you want a pair of my jeans?"

She felt her pulse quicken and chided herself, *Stop it, Kate. He's just trying to get on your good side by being generous.*

"No. I'll be all right." An unintentional shiver ran through her again.

He reached for the zip-up sweatshirt she'd hung on a bush before they'd begun work on the spring that morning. "I'll put some water on to heat, and run back to the spring for our shoes while it heats." He handed her the shirt. "Need some help?"

"No."

She put the sweatshirt on over her mud-splattered tee and huddled under the blanket again.

They sat on the ground beside the fire with hot chocolate Steve had made.

He cradled his warm mug in his hands. *She has no idea how cute she looks huddled under that blanket with her damp hair curling about her face.*

He took a sip from his cup and wiggled his bare toes in the warmth from the flames.

When she blushed and drew her own feet up under the blanket, he got up and donned a pair of canvas slippers.

He sat back down, resting his back against a log. "This reminds me of roasting hotdogs with my sister, Bet, when we were kids."

At the sound of ringing, his hand flew to his waist, but his phone wasn't there.

"It's mine." She pulled a cell phone from her sweatshirt

pocket, looked at the tiny screen and frowned. The phone rang again before she answered it. "Hello, Mother."

The crackle of a female voice issued from the phone. Kate held it away from her ear and frowned before placing it to her mouth again. "Aunt El doesn't try to keep track of me. *She* doesn't think she has to know where I am every minute."

He got up, poured himself another cup of hot chocolate and held the pot out toward Kate.

She shook her head and spoke into the phone. "Mother! She doesn't want me right under her feet. She told me to feel free to relax and do whatever I please."

She listened again. "I'm with—" she turned her back to him and lowered her voice "—a friend."

He smiled. Maybe they were finally getting somewhere.

"I was busy, Mother. I didn't have the phone with me." She took a deep breath and blew it out. "Yes, Mother, I'm fine. I'll try not to do anything else to make a fool of myself while I'm here." She paused. "Yeah, same to you. Bye."

Kate ended the call. When she turned around, he was putting another log on the fire. "My mother," she said, and wondered why she felt she needed to explain to him.

"Checking to be sure you're all right?"

"Checking to be sure I'm not doing something to embarrass her. I dumped my plate in my lap at Thanksgiving."

She saw him hide a grin but didn't care if he was laughing at her. It didn't matter what he thought. "I guess you saw the chocolate down the front of my shirt."

He just grinned.

"I had to get away before she started picking at me again. Like she did just now. She should have been a shrink."

"What do you have against therapists?"

"Nothing. I just don't want one picking at me." She narrowed her eyes at him. *I don't want you doing it, either.*

He studied her. "Has one ever…picked at you?"

"Mother took me once. I refused to go back."

"Does your mother know you're not returning to school?"

"It's my life. I can do what I want with it." She glanced around the clearing. "Including getting this place back. And camping out here while I fix up the house."

She stood and handed him the blanket. "Thanks. I have to go."

"You can't be dry yet." He stood. "Stay a while longer."

"I'm warm now. It won't matter if my clothes are a little damp." She stooped to put on her shoes.

"Take the blanket with you."

"No, thanks." She couldn't have Aunt El wondering where she came up with a blanket. She would look suspicious enough coming in with wet jeans.

"You can bring it back tomorrow. I'll go to church in the morning and have a meal afterwards. But I'll be here tomorrow afternoon."

Church? Where? She felt her eyes widen in alarm. What if it was her family's little church? And he spoke to her? How would she explain to them how she knew him? She needed to hurry up and figure out how to get her land back. This…relationship with *that man* was already getting too complicated for comfort.

Chapter 5

Kate slipped quietly into a back pew as the morning service began. She had driven her own car because her aunt and uncle were staying after the service for a fellowship dinner. She sure didn't want to encounter *him* at a social gathering.

Pulling a hymnal from its rack, she glanced round the sanctuary but didn't see him anywhere. He must have gone to the big church in town. Even as a sense of relief washed over her, something akin to disappointment settled in her chest.

She glanced round the sanctuary again.

No, no masculine head as dark as his, no unruly black beard.

She felt rather foolish thinking of all the time she had spent with the man without learning his name. But she wasn't about to give him the satisfaction of hearing her ask after she'd told him she didn't care to know. Her lawyer could probably find out for her, when—and if—he found a deed to the land, transferred from her mother and uncles to the man.

Kate's eyes shifted toward a pew near the front of the sanctuary where Aunt Ellendor and Uncle Rob sat. Uncle Sidney and his family sat behind them. On the far end of his pew sat their son Tom and three-year-old Tommy. A row of beautiful, poised women sat between them—Uncle Sid's wife, Nancy; their daughter Renae, the high school beauty queen; daughter Julia, whose husband was on a business trip; and Tom's wife, Susan. They were all singing, even little Tommy and Julia's four-year-old, Amy.

Kate held her songbook unopened on her lap as she noted the sheen on the row of smooth blond heads under the bright overhead lights. She reached up and smoothed her own wild mane. One more thing to show she was not like the rest of the family—in appearance, as well as interests.

She wouldn't mind being a little more like cousin Charlotte. Of course, she didn't care to go off to Asia as a missionary, but she would like a closer relationship with the Lord.

She just wasn't sure she could trust Him anymore.

Glancing toward the windows on the far side of the sanctuary, she saw the white gravestones glistening in the morning sun. She thought of the preacher's text on her first day back here. *I know the plans I have for you, says the Lord, plans to prosper you and not harm you, plans to give you a future and a hope.*

The man in the woods had quoted the same Scripture to her.

And I want to believe it, Lord. But how can I when things have turned out like this?

A picture of blue eyes crinkled at the corners and a dark head and beard popped into her mind.

She gritted her teeth. *No. I won't give in so easily to that insufferable man.*

She slid the hymnal into the rack and picked up her shoulder bag from the pew. She would trust the lawyer to find a way for her to get the land back.

In the meantime, she would enjoy the woods every chance she got. Maybe she could get to the campsite now and do a little sketching before *he* came in from church and lunch.

She slipped quietly from the pew and padded softly to the outer sanctuary doors.

Back at the house, she changed quickly into jeans and a gray-and-white long-sleeved flannel shirt. She tied her gray sweatshirt around her neck. Opening the refrigerator, she grabbed a bottle of water and the piece of chicken Aunt El had left for her. Then she stuck a sketch pad under her arm, pencils in a pocket and set out for the clearing in the woods, chewing on the cold chicken.

At the entrance to the campsite, she stopped short. That man sat at the table with a large sheet of paper spread out before him. Something akin to joy leaped inside her, but she quickly squelched it. Now she couldn't be alone with her drawing.

He looked up, saw her and smiled. "Come on in." He folded the paper, slipped it into a folder and placed the folder inside a large book lying on the table. He nodded toward the pad under her arm. "I see you brought something to read."

"It's a sketch pad."

"I didn't know you were an artist."

"I'm not. I just like to draw." She glanced toward the gnarled old tree with the outstretched limb. "I used to sit on that limb and sketch the trees and forest creatures. Before you turned it into a clothesline."

He grinned and held out a hand toward the tree, palm up. "Be my guest. I can remove the laundry." He made a move to stand.

"Never mind. I'll sit there later. After you've gone. When I'm *not* a guest."

He rolled his tongue around in his jaw and smoothed his beard, which had been neatly trimmed since yesterday. Long laugh lines ran down each cheek.

She turned her eyes from him and glanced toward the stream.

His gaze followed hers. "Did you want to rake now? The rakes are against the tree where we left them yesterday."

"No. I thought you might be at church and I'd have the place to myself."

He smiled. "Sorry to disappoint you. I went to early service."

"Oh. At the big church on the other side of town."

"A church near Birmingham where a friend of mine pastors."

The sudden chatter of a squirrel drew their attention to a nearby limb where the small creature sat scolding them. Kate glanced at the sketch pad in her hand.

"Go ahead and sit here at the table with your pad. I'll be quiet and let you work."

He probably hoped she'd be quiet and let him work. But he was the interloper here, not her.

"I'll sit over there." She nodded toward the scattered firewood.

Kate pulled a couple of pencils from a back pocket of her jeans, sat on a stick of firewood and folded her sweatshirt to cushion her back against a tree.

Maybe he should find another place to hang his laundry. Of course, she shouldn't be around much longer to see it. Surely she wouldn't quit school in her senior year to come back here and fight for the land.

When she opened the sketch pad and looked around

for something to draw, he smiled at her. With a toss of her bright head, she turned her face away.

But that was between her and her mama, he thought, certain she didn't want advice from him. He opened his notebook and picked up his pen. He had his own problems to work on, the main one being how he was going to get done all he needed to do here and at home, too. Especially if a smart-mouthed redhead continued to hang around.

He read a few pages, made a few notes in his notebook and glanced at her again. She was scratching away in the pad, lost in her sketching, seemingly unaware of his presence. He wished he could forget her as easily—the red hair flaming about her face, the fire in those gold-green eyes accusing him of— Of what? He'd paid good money for this place. She had no right to storm in here and accuse him of anything. Whatever the problem, it wasn't his.

But he couldn't forget her, and the other problems he sensed lying just below the surface of her anger and hostility. He was curious to know more about her. Learn what made her tick.

"Have you had art classes?"

She kept sketching. "A few. As electives. I'm studying— I *was studying* horticulture. And business. So I could start my own business."

She cast him an accusing look again.

He winced. "You can still operate your own business. If you finish your studies."

She made a few more scratches on the paper. "I practically run the garden shop where I work. I can operate my own business even if I don't go back to school. That is, I could if I had a place for one."

It was time to change the subject. "May I see what you're drawing?"

She turned the sketch pad around and waited without

comment for him to look at it. He stood and moved closer for a better view.

She had drawn a picture, a good likeness, of the snarled old tree—without his laundry strung on its branches. Her ability surprised him. "You're very good. It's a great likeness of the tree."

She tore the sheet out of the pad and handed it to him. "Here. Keep it to remind you of what it's supposed to look like."

He threw back his head and laughed.

She stood and brushed at the seat of her jeans. "I have to go."

"You just got here."

"And I'm just leaving."

She picked up her sweatshirt, stuck the pencils in a back pocket and left Steve scratching his beard.

Next morning, Kate dressed more carefully than usual in a white tailored shirt and brown slacks. She pulled her mop of hair back into a ponytail and secured it with a strong brown band. She wanted to run into town before donning jeans and heading for the woods to see what that man was doing.

She wanted to hurry and get him away from here. She'd left the campsite yesterday because of the way his nearness was beginning to affect her. The twinkle in his blue eyes and deep laugh lines down his cheeks when he grinned at her. It made her stomach queasy.

She didn't truly understand the feelings he stirred inside her, feelings that seemed inappropriate toward an adversary. But she'd had a stern talk with herself on the way back to the house and decided she would no longer allow him to affect her this way.

It was ridiculous, anyway, to let a man whose name she didn't even know run her out of her woods. Hopefully, this trip into town would supply her with a little ammunition against him. At least put a name to his face.

Outside the big oaken doors with the brass nameplate, she smoothed her ponytail and tucked her shirt more securely into the waistband of her slacks.

With her hand on the door handle, she took a deep breath and paused. She pictured her woods, her stream.

Lifting her head higher, she pushed open the door and looked around the sedate office. Jane, the pregnant administrative assistant, was nowhere in sight.

Then she saw the attorney bent over an open file drawer in the corner.

He had discarded his coat and tie. His brown hair, so perfectly groomed on her first visit, looked like he'd been running his hands through it.

He stood and looked at her. "Miss Sanderson! Do you know anything about filing systems?"

"Ye-yes, sir. I've been an office manager. And I've taken business courses."

A look of relief crossed the man's face. He let out an audible sigh of relief. "Do you think you might possibly help me locate a file?"

"I can try."

While Kate looked for the missing file, he talked on the telephone at the administrative assistant's desk. When she handed him the folder, he flipped through the papers, found what he needed and returned to the phone.

She turned her back to him and studied a painting on the wall.

"Miss Sanderson, I can't tell you how grateful I am."

She faced him.

"That was an important prospective client, and my assistant is home sick. I'm so accustomed to Jane's efficient assistance, I don't know how to find much around here without her."

He looked around the office, wearing a helpless expression. "Would you happen to know about word processing, too? And keeping records on the computer?"

"Yes. But…"

"If you know anything at all about computers and can spare the time this morning I would be very grateful if you could help me get a deposition ready…." He looked at the gold watch on his wrist. "I don't have time to look for anything on the computer. I have to be in court in an hour."

Kate backed off a step. Despite having a lawyer for a sister, she knew absolutely nothing about court documents.

"It's in the computer someplace," he said, looking confused again. "I have a hard copy Jane printed out and I edited. All you need to do is find it in the computer files, make the changes and print out a new copy." He glanced at his watch and heaved a sigh. "I'm running late again."

Kate looked at the computer on the desk, then back at the frustrated attorney.

I know the plans I have for you, plans to give you hope and a future.

Maybe you do have a plan here, God. I help him, he helps me.

"Miss Sanderson?"

Kate smiled. "No problem. I can handle it."

Half an hour later she carried the newly printed papers into his office. He sat at his desk with a pen in his hand.

He was again the sedate, impeccable attorney.

Kate stood with cupped hands before his desk, waiting while he read.

He looked up and nodded solemnly. "A good job. I'm sorry I didn't call to tell you about having to postpone your appointment."

He glanced at the stack of papers on the desk. "Miss Sanderson, I'm desperate and I know it sounds presumptuous, but since you're here anyway, could you stay awhile and answer the phones? I'm expecting an important call and I'd hate for a machine to take it or transfer it to my cell while I'm in court."

He was already standing, placing the papers Kate had printed into his briefcase, adjusting his tie. He picked up the papers from the desk. "Also, would you look up these files in the computer, make the corrections I've noted and reprint them?"

Kate stiffened. "Mr. Boyer, I'm hardly…"

"Yes, of course, Miss Sanderson. What was I thinking, asking you to spend the morning here?"

But the wheels were spinning in Kate's head. What would she lose by helping him? She may as well stay, and then hope when he returned he'd have some news for her.

"Mr. Boyer, I can help out. I'll be ready to talk when you get back."

He flashed her a relieved smile. "I'll come back around noon and check on things."

Kate reached for the papers. "No problem."

Shortly before Mr. Boyer returned from court, Jane called.

She seemed surprised but pleased to hear a female voice answer the telephone. She was having a problem with her pregnancy, she confided. She had been in bed all weekend and the doctor had told her to stay there a few more days.

"Will you be able to help out at the office while I'm away?" she asked anxiously. "I won't feel so bad about telling Mr. Boyer I have to be out if I know he has help."

A job, helping out a friend. She had met Jane only briefly, but she sounded friendly. This would give her a good excuse to stay here awhile longer, instead of returning to school.

She spoke into the phone again. "I think I can arrange that—if Mr. Boyer agrees."

"I'm sure he'll be pleased. And thank you. Call if you need me."

"Thanks." Kate smiled as she hung up the phone. She'd been wondering how she would get the money to pay legal fees.

The attorney proofed and okayed Kate's work when he rushed in at noon. He agreed, with a look of relief, for Kate to work while Jane was indisposed.

He turned toward his office with the stack of telephone messages Kate gave him.

"About Grandpa's land…"

"Let's talk about it in the morning."

Kate watched him disappear behind the paneled office door. *Okay, Mr. Boyer. If you say so. Just don't forget you're supposed to do something for me, too.*

She wondered if he'd have anything to tell her in the morning. It would make things easier if the intruder decided to run a closer check into his claim on the place. Maybe he'd find her mother had no right to sell it to him. Then he could get his money back and she could have her land.

When she stepped into the clearing late that afternoon, there was no sign of activity. The intruder was nowhere in sight. His blue mug sat on the picnic table and the dented, fire-blackened coffeepot rested on a flat stone inside the circle of rocks containing remnants of a burned-out campfire. But there were no books or clothing strewn about and the small tent was zipped up tight.

Her shoulders slumped. But she quickly straightened. *I'm glad he's gone. I just wish he had taken all his junk with him. He evidently plans to come back and…*

"What's that?" She squinted in the evening light.

Wooden stakes had been driven into the ground on a hill at the edge of the clearing. They appeared to form a square.

She stormed up the hill. He was staking out a building on her land! Even marking doorways and windows.

"I can't believe this. I just can't believe—"

She stopped speaking and stood with mouth agape as she remembered the large sheet of paper spread out on the table in front of the man when she'd walked into his camp on Sunday. When he'd seen Kate, he had quickly folded the paper and placed it inside a large folder.

She walked quickly back down the hill.

Unzipping the tent opening, she felt a slight twinge of guilt. But, after all, he was the intruder. If her lawyer wasn't going to do anything, she would have to.

She crawled through the tent opening, turned the flap back to let in light and sat down on the canvas floor looking around. Bedroll. Cooler. Box with food. Another with cooking supplies. Aha. That one must contain his books.

She crawled over to the plastic container and took off the lid. Books. She began pulling them out, searching for the one he'd placed the folder in. It wasn't there.

She glanced over the books scattered on the tent floor. *But here's something else that should be mighty useful.*

A book had fallen open to the fly leaf. And there, scrawled in bold letters, was a name.

Steve Adams.

She opened another book. *Stephen Q. Adams.*

Stephen. Steve. So that was his name. She nodded her head in satisfaction. She now had a name to give her lawyer.

She crawled from the tent, stood and stared at the wooden pegs sticking out of the ground on the hillside. Anger boiled inside her. "We'll just take care of that right now!"

She shed her sweatshirt and glanced around the camp area. She saw what she wanted leaning against a tree. Back up the hill she went, carrying Mr. Stephen Q. Adams's ax across her shoulder.

Chapter 6

Kate was waiting in the office parking lot when Mr. Boyer stepped from his black Lexus the next morning.

"Good morning, Miss Sanderson. We need to find you a key." He walked briskly to the back door.

Kate followed him in. "Mr. Boyer, I have the name of the man who says he bought Grandpa's land. If you…"

"Write it down and lay it on my desk." He glanced at the clock on the wall. "I have to get to court." He disappeared inside his office.

He reappeared in a few minutes and handed Kate a stack of letters she'd printed the day before. "These are all fine with the exception of one I needed to make changes on. After you've made them in the computer, you can reprint it and put them all in the mail. I have to run."

When he returned to the office a few hours later, he paused at Kate's desk for the mail. "Jane called," Kate told him. "She's feeling better and will be back tomorrow."

"Good. I appreciate your help these two days, but I'm glad she's better. I'll have her write a check for you."

"I thought we might apply it to my bill."

He glanced up from the paper in his hand and gave Kate a quizzical look.

"You know, for your helping me straighten out this mess about Grandpa's land."

"Uh, yes. Come into my office and we'll talk about that."

He turned toward his office as the back door opened.

"Paul, darling!"

A voluptuous blonde woman in heavy makeup and a sequined blouse breezed in from the parking lot. She sailed across the room toward the attorney, leaving a trail of perfume behind her.

A girl of about twelve with long brown hair and a long face followed the woman into the office and stopped just inside the door. When Kate smiled at her, she clamped her bottom lip between her teeth and turned her head.

The woman grabbed Mr. Boyer's hands and kissed his cheek. "I got in earlier than expected and went by and picked up Lisa. I asked Mrs. Mason to go ahead and cook dinner before she leaves. I thought we might all eat together tonight before I take the children with me for a few days. I have to return to Memphis for another conference at the end of the week."

"You ran out of money," Boyer said flatly, pulling his hands from hers.

The woman ignored his remark and beckoned to the child with a well-tanned hand tipped with red nails. "Come here, honey."

Lisa chewed her lip and ducked her head as she walked toward them. When her father put an arm around her, she leaned against his side.

"Have you seen Paul Jr.?" Mr. Boyer asked the woman.

"Mrs. Mason said he's at ball practice. I'll see him after she picks him up."

Mr. Boyer looked at Kate. "You haven't met my daughter, Miss Sanderson. This is Lisa and—her mother."

"Why, Paul, I didn't know you had a new administrative assistant." Mrs. Boyer appeared to see Kate for the first time. "Where is— What's the little pregnant girl's name?"

"Her name is Jane," Mr. Boyer answered drily. "She's been my assistant for five years, Claire."

"It's good to meet you, Jane," the woman said. She turned back to her husband, dismissing Kate.

"This is Miss Sanderson, Claire," Mr. Boyer said with a shake of his head. "She's helping me out while Jane is incapacitated."

"Oh." She glanced at Kate. "It's good to meet you, Miss Sanderson. I'm happy to know *someone* can help my husband."

"Ex-husband," the attorney muttered.

The attorney turned toward his office, one arm around his daughter. His ex-wife hung onto his other one.

At the door, he turned back. "Miss Sanderson, if you'll leave information about…the case we were discussing, I'll see what I can do. Make a note of anything you think might be helpful, and leave it in a folder on the desk. And be sure to leave an address for Jane to mail the check to you. And a phone number where I can reach you at the university."

Kate nodded. Maybe she *should* go back to school and finish the semester while the lawyer checked things. That should prevent at least one fight with her mother. And hopefully, by Christmas holidays, he would have some answers for her.

Steve looked around the clearing in the woods and shook his head. He'd think a raccoon had ransacked the place if it weren't for those markers. But as mischievous as the little creatures were, he hadn't met a coon yet that could dig up a stake that'd been hammered six inches into the ground, then chop it into splinters small enough to use for tooth picks. It had to be her.

Despite his irritation at the destruction of half a day's work when time was running short, he couldn't help smiling as he pictured her chopping away, her red hair flying.

He'd never known anyone quite like her. He sat down at the picnic table and unrolled the large sheet of paper in his hand. He was just glad he'd taken the plan with him. She would have shredded it.

He spread the drawing on the table but couldn't concentrate on it. Too many questions crowded his mind.

Had Kate's grandfather intended for her to have the place, but in his senility had failed to make proper arrangements? Had her family cheated her out of what was rightfully hers, as she seemed to believe? As an attorney, her sister could probably figure out a way to get around almost any law someone might wish to break. But would she? Perhaps if she were in on a shady deal.

Maybe he should do a little investigating on his own. He would hate to get a big project started only to have the place tied up in the courts.

He glanced at the hillside where his morning's work had been destroyed. He guessed he'd best let that project wait awhile and work on something else.

He pulled the collar of his jacket tighter around his neck and shivered. He needed to talk to Kate about this other idea that had been hatching in his head. The weather would soon be too cold for him to sleep comfortably in a tent.

He folded the drawing, laid it inside the tent and set about building a fire. As the stakes the woman had chopped to kindling ignited from an armful of dry pine straw, he thought about the Scripture verse he had quoted to her. *I know the plans I have for you, says the Lord...*

I thought I knew Your plans for me, Lord. Before she stormed into my camp and upset them all—the way she upset me from my makeshift stool and turned my life on its head.

Kate drove back to school on Tuesday evening. She heard loud music playing as she lugged her bags up the stairs to her apartment on the second floor. Somewhere down the hall, someone banged on the wall. "Turn it down, will ya! I'm trying to study in here."

Her tiny apartment seemed claustrophobic after the openness of the woods and her aunt's spacious house. And very lonely, despite all the noise. She had come close to thinking of it as home before going back to a real home. Now the cheap, worn sofa bed, small rickety table, ancient gas stove and stained bathtub seemed strange to her.

While working and attending classes, she had made few friends on campus, not one she could call a close friend or confidante. There was no one to call just to say "I'm back." There was nobody to care whether or not she came back.

Except maybe Mrs. Adelle, her employer at the garden shop. She needed to give her a call to let her know she could come to work when needed. She'd do that soon as she unpacked the few groceries she'd picked up at Winn-Dixie.

"Thank goodness you're back," the elderly shop owner exclaimed when Kate called. "I've missed your help with the plants."

Kate smiled into the phone. It was nice to know someone missed her, even if it was only because she needed her help.

Kate assured her boss she would be at work the next day, since her only classes this week were on Thursday and Friday. Aunt El had told her she was welcome to stay at her house anytime, and she'd been tempted to return for the weekend. But semester finals were a week away and she needed to study and work a few shifts at the garden shop to help pay expenses.

She liked earning her own money and being able to tuck a few dollars into Aunt El's canister, where she kept her grocery money.

Passing the one little window, she saw a girl and guy playing football on the grass below. The girl squealed as she tackled him and they both landed on the ground.

Kate thought about the day she'd attempted to push Steve into the stream and fell in herself. She hugged herself and gave a delicious little shiver recalling the way he'd held her to warm her. He really didn't seem like a bad person, not like someone who would just move in and take over a place without legal right to it.

Maybe Mr. Boyer could help her get the land problem straightened out before Steve laid out his building again and started construction. She really didn't want to hurt the man, nor fight with him. She just wanted her land back.

With a deep sigh, Kate turned from the window, opened the refrigerator door and pulled out the milk. When she walked back to the table for cereal and peanut butter, the couple were standing, wrapped in each other's arms, laughing.

Would she ever have this kind of relationship with anyone? She sighed and pulled her accounting textbook from her bag. If she could get her degree *and* her land back, she wouldn't need a relationship—she'd have everything she needed.

Chapter 7

"Jane's doctor told her to work only half days for a while," Kate told the attorney when he walked into the office and found her sitting at Jane's desk. "She asked me to work in her place for a few days while I'm out of school for Christmas holidays. I hope that's all right."

He nodded. "That's fine. However you two can work it out. I just need someone who can do the job and be here when I'm in court." He set his briefcase beside the desk and picked up a stack of letters Kate had printed.

"Did you learn anything about the sale of my family's property while I was gone?" she asked.

"Well, uh— I did find where your mother and uncles deeded the property in question to Stephen Adams, but no record of your grandfather deeding it to anyone."

He glanced at the letters. "I'll take these to my office and sign them."

"What about a Last Will and Testament?"

"I'll check on it."

He'd check on it? She couldn't believe a lawyer hadn't thought to look for a will. She heaved a deep sigh as his office door closed behind him. *Well, maybe tomorrow.*

But he rushed off to court next morning and had not returned when Jane arrived at noon.

Kate hurried out to her car in a flurry of golden maple leaves from trees lining the parking lot. With Christmas less than three weeks away, this wonderful autumn weather wouldn't last long. By the look of clouds in the distance, rain was already on the way. It was sure to bring cold weather. She would grab a burger, hurry home and head for the woods with her pad and pencil.

Hopefully that infuriating man would not be there, and she could spend a few relaxing moments alone.

If Mr. Boyer kept fooling around about checking on her rights to the land, she would go to the county courthouse and check records herself.

Falling leaves swirled about Steve's pickup as he drove down the little town's main street, but he barely noticed. His mind was taken up with what he'd just discovered at the county courthouse.

He glanced at the paper lying on the truck seat beside him. Kate would be devastated.

What should he do with the paper? File it away and wait to see what transpired? Or try to talk to her about it? Maybe he...

His foot spontaneously flew to the brake. He whirled to look behind him. Was that Kate pulling out of that parking lot?

A horn honked, yanking his attention back to his driving.

He glanced in the rearview mirror. A moving van blocked his view.

Nah, probably not her. What if it was? Would he jump

out in traffic and wave her down with the paper just so he could prove he owned the land?

No, he wouldn't be the one to break her heart with the truth. He'd let someone else be the culprit. The best he could do was try to be around to help pick up the pieces when she found out.

He glanced in the mirror again. No sign of her blue Escort. He'd seen no sign of her for over a week. She was probably at Auburn studying for exams. He was glad she was continuing her education, but surprised she would leave here for so long when she seemed determined to find a way to get the land back. And keep him from building on it in the meantime.

He couldn't help but smile every time he thought about her digging up his stakes.

Glancing round the deserted campsite, Kate felt an emptiness in her chest. Had he finally realized she wasn't giving up this place without a fight?

No, he wouldn't leave if he had a clear title. He wouldn't give up easily, either.

Well, she would enjoy the place while she had opportunity. If she didn't freeze out here. The weather was much cooler than when she'd left for school.

Using both hands, she hoisted herself up to straddle the tree limb the intruder had used to dry his laundry on, the limb where she'd spent many happy hours reading and sketching. She moved backward until her back touched the tree trunk, then pulled the sketch pad from her waistband and the pencil from her ponytail. She drew up her right foot and propped it on the limb in front of her. Her left foot dangled beneath the branch as she leaned back against the tree and opened the pad.

From her perch, she watched squirrels dart from tree to ground to tree, gathering and storing the remains of the oak and hickory trees' bounty. A breeze stirred the wisps of hair escaping her ponytail holder and blew a shower of color down around her. She smiled and touched pencil to paper.

But the marks she made were…only marks. Not because the small creatures moved about too quickly for her to capture them on paper. She'd never had problems with that before, at least not before that man had come.

Leaning her head back against the rough bark of the tree trunk, she closed her eyes and sighed. How she wished this thing was cleared up and that man gone, so she could get her life back.

She opened her eyes. Sat and doodled on the pad while glancing around the clearing hoping to recapture a sense of earlier times, when life was simpler—and less confusing. Instead, she found Steve's presence haunting the place. It didn't matter that his belongings were gone—*he* was still there. His laughter. His voice. His dark hair curling around his ear. Square chin with dark beard, blue eyes crinkling at the corners as…

"No! I will not let you take over here, Stephen Q. Adams—in body or in spirit! I refuse to let you."

She ripped the sheet from the pad and was about to wad it in her hand when she noticed a face among her doodling. Steve Adams smiled up at her!

"No!" She wadded it up and threw the balled paper onto the ground. "You will not invade my life this way."

And just at that moment she heard a deep, male voice echoing through the trees. It seemed to come from the patch of woods between the clearing and farmhouse.

"'Coming home…'" The man was singing an old hymn to the accompaniment of a strange thumping sound. "'Never more to roam…'" *(thumpety, thump, thump)* "'Open wide those pearly gates'" *(thumpety, thump, thump)*…

Was he beating a drum while he sang?

As she listened, the noise grew louder. He was headed her way!

Instinctively, she drew up the leg dangling below the limb. She glanced down at the wadded paper on the ground and then toward the trail through the trees. There was no denying whose likeness she had drawn. Did she have time to climb down and retrieve it before he got there and saw it? Or should she try climbing higher and hide among the leaves? And pray the rain would come and erase the picture before he discovered it?

She swiveled her head around to look up into the tree.

And dropped the sketch pad.

Loose papers flew from the pad. These, he *couldn't* miss.

She glanced toward the trail through the woods, then at the ground. It appeared much farther down than it was up. Could she jump without jarring her teeth out of her head?

The singing and bumping grew louder. They were getting closer. There was no time to do anything but jump.

Frantically, she tried to maneuver into position to swing down from the tree. But as she attempted to slide her right leg off the limb, her jeans caught on a snag.

The jolt yanked her left hand from the limb, and she was left hanging. Her right leg and arm held her to the tree while her left leg and arm dangled below her.

Suddenly, the singing stopped.

The bumping grew louder and faster.

She strained to look behind her, to see where it was coming from. All she could see was a blur moving fast toward her. It was beneath the limb where she hung when her grip gave way.

And she fell with a thud.

"Ugh!" His arms closed round her as the breath was knocked out of him.

She pushed his arms away and jumped to her feet. "Were you trying to catch me in a *wheelbarrow?*" She stared in disbelief at the contraption he had pushed ahead of him as he'd run to catch her.

He stared up at her through a streak of sunlight slanting through the trees. He gasped for breath. "I didn't…realize I was still…pushing it." He struggled to his feet, laughing between gasps.

"What are you doing with it anyway? It's not enough to trespass here, you have to steal the dirt, too?"

She'd lost her ponytail holder in her fall and her hair fanned out about her. But she didn't care how she looked to him or how hard he laughed at her. She had more important things to think about. She had to keep him from realizing what she was doing in the tree and noticing the papers on the ground.

But he wasn't letting her off so easily—he recognized that she was trying to divert his attention from her plight. "Maybe I should ask what you were doing swinging from my clothesline."

"Huh?"

Kate glanced up at the tree limb and then laughed with him, even as she recalled his laundry spread on her tree to dry.

She had to admit she must have been a funny sight dangling from the tree limb. And he had, after all, rushed to save her. "Did I hurt you?" She hoped she had—a little bit, anyway.

Still grinning, he rubbed his midsection. "I think you gave me a hernia."

She stooped and picked up the pages from her sketch pad. She didn't look at him as she wadded and stuffed them into her pocket and then picked up the band that had secured her ponytail. "Maybe it will stop you from loading that wheelbarrow with my dirt."

"I didn't come for dirt. I came…" He stopped.

"Yes?" She looked up at him, waiting for him to finish.

The smile left his face. He took her arm to help her to her feet.

She yanked her arm away and reached up to pull back her tangled hair. His arms around her unnerved her more than the fall, but she couldn't let him know that. She didn't want to know it herself.

"Come sit at the table. I want to talk to you about something."

She watched him limp to the table, a hand to his back. Did he intend to scold her for chopping up the stakes he'd used to lay out his house? Just let him try. She'd tell him a few things, too.

She followed him to the table and slid onto the bench across from him. "Well?"

He just stared at her with a sad sparkle in his eye, and again she found herself noting his kindness. *Forget it. I can't let him distract me from the prize.* Firmly resolved, she met his eye and waited for him to continue.

Chapter 8

Steve could tell by Kate's hostile glare this wasn't going to be easy.

"Well? What did you want to say to me?"

She shivered in a sudden cool breeze, giving him his opening. "It's getting cooler. And, according to the weatherman, rain is on the way."

"That's why you wanted to talk to me—to give me a weather report?"

He grinned. She was good with a quick comeback, all right. "Actually, I wanted to ask you something about the old house."

"What about it?" She eyed him with suspicion.

"Since it will soon be too cold to camp out, I thought I might fix up the house enough to stay in it for a while. What do you think?"

"No." Her chin lifted and her nostrils flared. Then she slumped on the bench as the fight went out of her. "Why are you asking *me?* You didn't ask me before you came in here and took over the land."

He squelched the urge to reach out and take her hand. "That was before I met you."

She caught her bottom lip between her teeth and lowered her head. A tear dropped from under the screen of her hair.

Steve, you're a louse. He reached across the table and touched her cheek.

When she didn't pull back, he rubbed away her tears with the tips of his fingers. "I'm sorry. I know this is difficult for you."

She leaned her face into his touch. But only for a second before she pushed his hand away and sat up straight. "You don't need to ask my permission, if you own the place like you say."

"Will you walk to the house with me to look at it?"

"Why?"

"I'd like your opinion on some things. I want to see what you'd like to keep. If there's anything salvageable."

"I don't have a place to keep anything."

"You can tell me if there's something you want and I'll hold it for you."

"How about the house itself?" She glanced around them. "And this little piece of land?" She jumped to her feet. "Never mind. We'll get to that later. It's getting cool out here. We'd best be going to the house, if we're going."

She kept her eyes averted from him as they walked along the path toward the house. Her cheek still tingled from his touch. She was sure both cheeks must be pink. What in the world had caused her to lean her face against his hand anyway? It wasn't as though she wanted sympathy or comfort from *him.* He was the last person in the world she would turn to. After all, he was the one causing her misery.

When they reached the edge of the wooded area, he stopped. "Look! There, under the big oak." A sleek reddish-brown doe munched acorns at the edge of the yard.

Kate felt a smile cross her face. "I've seen deer come right up to the edge of the house. We used to put out fruit and vegetable scraps for them."

They stood quietly until the deer threw up her short white tail and bolted into the trees.

He laughed softly. "We spooked her, invading her territory this way."

"I know how she feels."

"Let's go round to the front. The back steps need to be repaired, but I replaced the missing boards on the front porch. And I tacked a temporary covering over the hole in the roof."

She nodded for him to go first along the trail he had trampled through the grass.

When they reached the front door, Steve pushed it open and stepped aside for Kate to enter.

She stopped on the threshold.

He waited silently from several steps behind her while she glanced around the room. She knew he was giving her time to adjust emotionally to the changes. And she was grateful.

"This was Grandpa's living room. Or 'the parlor,' as Grandmother used to call it. She was a society girl from up north, you know."

"No, I didn't know."

"She met Grandpa while he was stationed up there with the army."

"That's interesting." He sounded as if he really meant it. But she didn't need to go into that just now. Taking a deep breath, she caught her bottom lip between her teeth and stepped into the room.

He followed close behind her and laid a gentle hand on her shoulder.

She let it rest there. She needed a human touch just now. Even if it was his.

Steve sensed her pain and wanted to offer comfort. When she didn't flinch, he was tempted to pull her into his arms but was afraid she would misread his intentions.

So he gave her shoulder an understanding pat and then stepped back to watch as she walked slowly around the room.

She trailed a finger through a thick layer of dust on the small round table beside a leather easy chair. She touched the rocker beside the fireplace and started it rocking. She patted a molding sofa cushion.

When she came to the desk, she stopped. "This is where I found Grandpa the day of his big stroke. He was sprawled here on the floor."

She blinked away tears as she moved to the fireplace. "The chimney will need to be cleaned out before a fire is built in it."

"Will you help me clean it?" Working on the place might be good therapy for her.

She shrugged. "Why not?"

"I'll go outside and find something to work with." He would give her a little time alone inside, and then maybe he could distract her while she was halfway agreeable— before her emotions got the best of her. She looked as though she was about to break into tears.

When he came back inside, she appeared to have herself under control.

He used a cane pole he found under the front porch to dislodge an old bird's nest, leaves and pine cones from the chimney. Then she helped him gather fallen limbs and sticks to build a fire in the fireplace. Neither of them seemed to have lasting injuries from her fall on top of him.

Standing with backs to the fire they built in the old stone fireplace, her gaze swept the room. A lone tear trickled down one cheek. Instinctively, before he realized what he was doing, he reached out and enfolded her in his arms.

She rested her forehead against his chin, and he thought for a moment she was going to hug him, too. But as soon as her arms slipped around his waist, she pulled them back. "I'm—all right. Thank you."

He let her go and was surprised to realize he wanted to hold her longer. Not for her this time, but for him.

She took a deep breath and wiped her face on the sleeve of her sweatshirt. "The sofa will need to be cleaned and aired and the curtains thrown away. Grandmother had the room done up really pretty. But Grandpa and I decided it was too fancy for our lifestyle after she was gone. We took down the lace curtains and put up these plain red ones and covered the brocade sofa with that heavy woven material."

She studied the sofa a minute. "If those covers are too far gone, we might be able to pull them off to check the brocade underneath. It still looked good when we covered it up. Of course, that was several years ago."

"How old were you when your grandmother died?"

"Eleven." She dropped into the dusty rocker.

He sat down on the hearth. "Do you miss her?"

She shook her head. "No. I always felt guilty because I didn't hate to see her go. She was real fussy about everything, always worrying about what people think and criticizing Grandpa and me. I guess that's where Mother gets it."

She glanced round the room again. "We kept intending to repaper the walls but never got around to it. When the stroke sent him to the nursing home, there were only a few small tears in the paper and that big one over the desk where he tore it moving the desk around."

She sprang to her feet. "Speaking of fixing up, we'd best get busy if you're going to sleep here after the rain starts."

Steve smothered a smile and stood. Better get at it while Kate was in the mood.

Later that evening, Kate cradled a heavy mug in her hands and sniffed the rich aroma of hot chocolate mingled with the scent of burning hickory. The fire in the grate hissed and spewed as blue-and-yellow flames leaped up the blackened chimney. She looked at the man sitting beside her on the sofa.

Firelight played across his face as he glanced around the room and then at her. He smiled, white teeth glistening through the dark beard. "We got a lot done." He patted a sofa cushion. "The sofa cleaned up quite well. I think I'll sleep on it tonight."

He settled back and crossed his legs. His knee almost touched Kate's as he rested his ankle on the other knee. She stood, careful not to touch him. "I think I'd better go. It'll soon be dark."

"I'll drive you in the pickup." He rose to his feet, in no rush to get his keys.

"I'll walk through the woods. There's plenty of light yet. I've walked the trail many times when it was later than this." She didn't want anyone seeing her in the pickup with him.

He walked outside with her. "Do you want to come back tomorrow? You haven't told me what you want to keep."

What she wanted to keep? She didn't want anything right now. She wanted everything left as is until she decided how she wanted things when she started her business. It was the intruder she wanted out. "I'll be at work."

"Work? You're working here in town?" He looked startled. "When I didn't see you for a while I thought you were at school."

"I went back for finals, but I'm working now at—an office in town."

"Do you want to stop by after work tomorrow? I'll make soup."

Whether she came or didn't, she knew he would be here working on the house. She may as well stick around and see what he was doing to it. Besides, with his help, she would be further ahead with cleaning once the legal details were straightened out and she got the place back.

"I get off at noon."

"Good. Come on by."

"Maybe I will—to be sure you're not destroying things." She turned and hurried away before he could comment.

But not before she saw him smile.

A steady drizzle started the next day just after Kate left the office at noon. She went by the house to change into jeans, found Aunt El cleaning and helped with the vacuuming before driving over to the old house.

By the time she reached the driveway leading to the farmhouse, it was early evening. She stopped and peered through the wet windshield. Gravel filled the ditches. The boulders had been moved out of the road. It seemed safe to try driving.

As she pulled up in front of the house, Steve ran down the steps with an open umbrella. He held it over her as she stepped from the car.

"I built a fire to dry us out." He put an arm around her shoulders and leaned his head close to hers as they hurried to the porch. His warm breath tickled her ear.

She pulled away from him when they stepped up on the porch.

The smell of cooking tomatoes, mingling with other vegetables, greeted them as he opened the door, and she breathed in hungrily. It smelled like Grandpa still lived here.

"Grandpa used to make vegetable soup, too. No one can make it like he did." She brushed past him and went inside.

"Don't knock it till you've tried it." A grin tilted the edges of his mouth.

"Not knocking it. Just stating facts." She walked to the fireplace and sat in the rocker.

He headed for the kitchen. "I'll bring bowls in here and we can eat by the fire. You can put your shoes by the hearth to dry, if you'd like."

She would like to do just that. She had often sat beside this very hearth and wiggled her toes in the warmth of a crackling fire. But she couldn't do anything that personal around him.

For the first time, suspicions about his intentions toward her—other than to take her land—crossed her mind.

"Here you go. Try it. I think you'll like it."

She jumped and looked at him, her cheeks burning. But not from the fire. How foolish to think a man who looked like this one would try to force his attention on *her*. He probably had women—glamorous ones like her sister and cousins—falling all over him every place he went.

Maybe she should stop being so negative. Or he wouldn't want her around. To help with the cleaning, of course.

She smiled at him as she took a bowl from the tray he held. "Thank you."

He set the tray on the hearth. It held a second bowl, two wedges of corn bread and two glasses of milk.

"I have coffee to go with the pie."

"Pie? You made pie, too?"

He grinned. "From the grocery store deli—like the bread. I still have to learn how to deal with that oven."

"Yeah, it's temperamental." She picked up a wedge of corn bread.

He quirked an eyebrow at her and grinned.

She gave a short laugh. "Go ahead and say it. The oven takes after me."

His grin broadened. "You said it, I didn't."

They laughed together. It felt good. If only there wasn't this thing about the land between them, she could really enjoy being around him.

He pulled up a footstool and sat down. "You want to say grace, or want me to?"

"You go ahead." She bowed her head.

They ate in companionable silence, like the day they'd worked on the spring together. She smiled to herself when he broke a piece off his corn bread and crumbled it in his soup. She had resisted doing the same, not wanting to appear too country.

He grinned. "I like seeing a woman enjoy her soup. Especially when I cook it."

"It is pretty good. Passable, anyway."

He gave an amused grunt. "You only build me up to let me down."

She bit back a snippy retort. They could probably get a lot more done if they were not always at odds with each other. There was really no reason to be angry with him anyway. He had bought and paid for the land. Mr. Boyer had found a deed signing the place over to him. He couldn't control how her mother and uncles came by it.

She munched a bite of bread while she thought about it. Maybe she should let him know a lawyer was checking on it for her. She turned her gaze from the fire and looked at him. His dark hair glistened in the firelight.

She wondered how old he was. What kind of work did he do? He must not do much of anything since he was down here so much.

"Do I pass inspection?"

Her cheeks grew hot. She hadn't realized he was watching her. She lifted her chin and leveled a look down her nose. "I was wondering how long an employer will allow a person to hide out in the woods."

"Maybe the *person* doesn't have an employer."

"Maybe." She studied him. "But how does this *person* without an employer earn a living?"

"Well, he could be an employer instead of an employee. He could have a family who supports him. He could be independently wealthy."

"Even employers have to work sometimes. And I've never seen a preacher who was paid enough to support an overgrown son who doesn't work. And if I'm not mistaken, you said your father was a minister. So it must be the last one. Are you a multimillionaire?"

He threw back his head and laughed. "Far from it."

Another thought struck her. He said a *family* who supports him, not a *father*. Maybe he had a wife who supported him. "Do you— Is there a—Mrs. Stephen Adams?"

His eyebrows shot up. "How long have you known?"

"You're—married?" Her heart plummeted.

He laughed. "I meant how long have you known my name."

"Oh, that. I've known it forever."

"You have not."

"Yes, I have. For a long time, anyway. Do you think I'd be eating homemade soup in front of a crackling fire with a man whose name I don't even know?"

"You didn't let me know you knew."

And you didn't answer my question. She chewed her lip as she studied him. Why would he not tell her if he had a wife? He still had not told her whom he'd been talking about that day in the woods when he'd said *we* were going to have horses here.

"When you get through inspecting me, you need to finish your soup so we can have pie."

She didn't return his grin. "I went to see an attorney."

He nodded.

"You already knew?"

"I saw you."

"Saw me!" She jumped to her feet and handed him the bowl. "Thanks for the supper, Mr. Adams. I'm afraid I must leave. I have to go to work early in the morning. *At my job in the attorney's office.*"

"Oh. So that's why you were there."

"And why did you think I was there?"

She knew what he thought. And he was right about why she had gone to the lawyer's office to start with. But he had no right spying on her.

Steve stared at her. The lawyer must have told her about the deed. Her temper sparked as hot as the fire in the grate, as bright as the flames of red-and-gold hair cascading about her face. He couldn't tell if reflection from the fire or the fire in her eyes shot flames at him.

But why was she angry at *him?* What had he done to set her off this time? He couldn't help what had happened long before he'd come on the scene, couldn't help what her grandfather had done. Surely she understood that. He wanted to grab her and shake her. He wanted to grab her and kiss the anger and hostility out of her. He clenched his hands at his sides to keep them off her.

"Well, why? Why did you think I was at a lawyer's office? You thought I was there looking for a way to get my land back, didn't you?"

He unclenched his hands. How was he to answer her? For a while he *had* thought she might find a way to get the land. That her grandfather really had left at least a part of it to her. Then he'd seen the record—and was still puzzling over it.

Kate dropped back into the chair. "If I were in your shoes, I might spy on you, too."

He relaxed and grinned at her. "Like you did after the first time you saw me in the woods?"

"I didn't."

"You did, too."

A smile lit her eyes. "Okay. Maybe you caught me on that one. Maybe I shouldn't accuse you. So tell me how you happened to see me in the lawyer's office."

"I didn't see you *in* it. I drove by as you were leaving."

"Oh."

She was more subdued as she spooned the last bite of soup from her bowl and took the last bite of bread.

"You ready for pie now? I'll put a couple slices in the microwave." He reached for her bowl.

"Sounds good." She smiled at him as she placed her spoon in the bowl and handed it to him.

He returned her smile. "Two slices of warm apple pie coming right up."

At the kitchen doorway, he hesitated and almost turned back. He hated keeping things from her and wanted to tell her about his trip to the courthouse.

But he had a feeling she wasn't telling him everything, either. Without comment he continued into the kitchen to warm their pie.

Chapter 9

Kate turned from the computer and reached for the ringing telephone. "Paul Boyer's office."

"Kate. The doctor's putting me on bed rest again."

"Oh, Jane, I'm sorry."

"Can you work full-time for a while? You can call me for help or bring things by my house, if you need to. I'll talk to Mr. Boyer about it."

"I'll be going back to school after the holidays." *If I go back*.

"Maybe I can be back in the office part-time by then. But can you work every day until then?"

"I…don't know." If she worked all day every day, when could she check on what was going on in the house and woods? When could she help work on the place?

I know the plans I have for you…plans to prosper you, to give you a future and a hope.

Kate thought about the way the Scripture kept returning to her mind. Could she trust it? Did she believe what the Bible said? She grew up believing every word in the Bible—although she didn't understand it all. Could she stop believing just because she couldn't understand all the things going on around her or how the verse could possibly apply to her life now?

She took a deep breath and decided to take the plunge. "All right, Jane, I'll do it. If Mr. Boyer agrees."

"Great. I'm sure he'll be happy to have you. If he's there let me talk to him a minute."

After talking with Jane, the attorney walked into the office where Kate worked at the computer. "Jane says you are able to work while she's incapacitated and call her if you need to."

"Yes, sir."

"Good." He handed her the letter he'd signed. "Please see that it gets in the afternoon mail."

Kate reached for the letter as the front door opened. A boy of about ten dragged into the office, head down, hands dangling at his sides.

Paul Boyer turned to look at him. "Pauley, what are you doing here?"

"You missed my game again." He let his backpack slip from his shoulders to the floor.

"I'm sorry, Paul Jr. I got caught up in court."

Kate felt her eyes widen. *Not true, Mr. Boyer.*

Paul Jr. slumped into a chair. "That's okay, Dad. We lost anyway."

"How did you get here from the game? It will be a while before I can go home."

"Joel's mom dropped me off. I'll wait." He propped his chin in his hands and stared at the floor.

Kate's heart went out to him. She could well understand how he felt, being ignored by the people he loved most. She wished she could do something to make him feel better.

The phone rang, and Mr. Boyer stood silently waiting while she answered it.

She held her hand over the mouthpiece. "It's Lucas Oswald, about the Walters case. Should I tell him you'll call him back?" She nodded toward the desolate boy.

Boyer glanced at his son and frowned. "No, I'd better talk to him now. I'll take it in my office."

After the door closed behind him, Kate looked at the boy. He still sat slumped over, his head down.

"Paul Jr.?"

"Yeah?" He didn't look at her.

"You like chocolate cake?"

He shrugged without looking up. "Yeah."

"I have a piece in my desk drawer. You want to share it?"

He looked up, interest lighting his eyes. "You got enough?"

"I have plenty."

"Okay." He got up and ambled toward her.

Kate opened a desk drawer, took out a covered plastic container and set it on the desk. She lifted her shoulder bag and opened it. "You want to run next door to the barbershop and get drinks from their machine?"

"Sure."

She smiled and handed him a couple of bills. "I'll take anything diet. Get whatever you want. I think they have a snack machine, too. Get a package of crackers, if you'd like. It may be a while before your dad's ready to go."

While Paul Jr. was gone, she opened the container and sliced off a tiny corner from the cake wedge. Leaving it in the container where the boy couldn't see how small it was, she placed the larger portion on a paper plate for him. She got up and pulled a chair near the desk.

Paul Jr. returned carrying a couple of soft drinks in cans. "Diet cola okay?"

"That's great. Have a seat." She indicated the chair across the desk from her.

The boy sat down, and Kate placed the plate in front of him.

He picked up his plastic fork and dug in. "Wow! This is good." He spoke with his mouth full. "Did you make it?"

"Sure did." She took a tiny bite with her plastic fork.

He took another bite. "I wish my mom made cakes like this." He bit his bottom lip. Chocolate coated his teeth. "I wish she stayed around long enough to make one."

"Tell me about your game."

Gloom surrounded the boy again. "I missed a free throw. If I hadn't we would've won the game."

"Oh, I'm sure you're not the only one who failed to get a basket."

"I scored two times," he said eagerly, then slumped in the chair again. "But Jason Phillips scored lots more. He made *eight* baskets."

He tilted his head to one side and studied Kate. "Do you play? You're tall."

"I'm afraid not. I have a brother who plays, though. He's in high school. He plays all sorts of sports."

"Is he good?"

"Pretty good. He's won some trophies."

"Does he live around here? Maybe he could play with me sometime. My dad's always too busy." He stuffed another bite of cake into his mouth. "This sure is good."

"Thank you." Kate smiled and took a tiny bite as the door opened from the inner office.

Paul Boyer walked out with a sheaf of papers in his hand.

"Look, Dad. Kate can make chocolate cake."

Boyer cocked an eyebrow at his son. "*Kate* can make chocolate cake?"

"Yeah. It's real good, too. You want a bite?"

"Not now, son." Kate's boss looked at her and smiled.

"Maybe Kate will make another cake soon. And share it, too."

He nodded at her and turned back to the boy.

She stared at his back. That was the first time he'd ever called her anything except Miss Sanderson. And he had never smiled at her that way before.

She would try to bake another cake before long. If his son didn't get homemade goodies, he probably didn't, either.

Unless he was like the man staying in her house, and cooked for himself.

She wondered what Steve was cooking for supper tonight. Maybe she'd stop by on her way home and find out.

"Dad, there's another game Saturday morning. Can you go?"

Kate's attention was drawn back to father and son. She watched the man's face scrunch into a frown. "Oh, son, I've just made an appointment for Saturday morning."

"Can't you change it?"

"I'm afraid not. This appointment is with a *very* important client."

Aren't they all?

Paul Boyer turned away from his son as he studied the papers in his hand. The boy's face crumpled. Before she realized what she was about to say, Kate asked, "Do you think I could go watch you play?"

Paul Jr.'s head jerked up, a look of surprised joy on his face. "Would you really come to my game? Mom will be busy, too."

"I'd love to." Despite her aversion to organized sports, she would like to go watch his game. If only to please him, and so he would know there was someone there to watch only him. She smiled at the grinning child.

His father looked at her, frowning. "You don't have to do that."

"I don't mind. If you don't."

"Oh, no. I would appreciate it—seeing as how neither his mother nor I will be able to go." He studied her over the top of the papers he held.

Flustered by his scrutiny, she turned back to the computer screen.

Her boss cleared his throat. "I hope you appreciate what Kate—Miss Sanderson—is doing, son, giving up her Saturday morning to go with you."

"Sure, Dad. She's great, ain't she?"

"*Isn't* she, son. *Isn't* she."

"Yeah. I'm glad you think so, too, Dad."

Kate suppressed a smile as she heard Mr. Boyer's grunt just before his office door opened then closed again. She turned and winked at Paul Jr.

"What?" He glanced around him. "What?"

"Nothing. Eat your cake."

Steve set his supper plate on the hearth and lifted a large stick of firewood from the chimney corner. He placed the wood in the fireplace and was arranging it on the fire with the poker when he heard a car door slam. Kate?

He grabbed an umbrella from its stand and hurried to open the door.

She was hurrying up the steps, huddled inside a dark hooded jacket. "It's not raining anymore," she said. "Just turning cold."

He opened the door wider. "Come on in. I built a fire."

She went to the hearth and held her hands toward the flames.

"I've been trying to tame that oven," he said. "I baked a couple of chicken breasts. One for you, if you want it."

She eyed the plate on the hearth. "Okay."

"You want rice and a salad?"

"Sure."

When he returned to the room, she had removed her

jacket and hung it on the old coatrack by the door. She was running her hand along the base of the rack, caressing the time-darkened wood.

"That's a fine piece of craftsmanship. Did your grandfather make it?"

"Yes. He made it for my grandmother before I was born."

"You can take it if you like." He set her plate and a glass of tea on the small round table by the rocker. "Here, help yourself. I thought we would eat in here by the fire."

After his short prayer over the food, they cut into the chicken breasts.

"I found an old trunk in the barn," he said. "It's full of Christmas decorations. I thought we might use them to trim a tree."

"Help yourself." She forked a bite of chicken into her mouth.

"It won't be any fun by myself. I thought you might help. Could you come Saturday morning and look for a tree with me?"

"I'm busy Saturday morning. Going to a basketball game." She cut another bite of chicken.

"A ball game? Sounds like fun. Around here?"

"Over at the school gym. A bunch of little kids."

She didn't take the hint and invite him along. Probably didn't want to be seen around town with him, with his scraggly beard and ratty jeans.

He suppressed a smile. He'd have to show her how nicely he cleaned up sometime. "I thought you told me you don't like sports."

She shrugged. "I told one of the boys on the team that I'd come watch him play." She bent back to her plate.

"A brother? Nephew?" He gave her a teasing grin. "A son?"

"Yeah. A son. My boss's son."

"Oh. You gave me a jolt there for a second. I thought you meant *your* son."

She looked up with a frown. "Why would that surprise you?"

He chuckled. "A son old enough to play basketball? You would have been—what? Maybe thirteen at the most when he was born?"

She shrugged. "Who's counting?"

"Me?"

She laughed.

"Do you want to come by and look for the tree Saturday afternoon instead of Saturday morning? Should be a little warmer by then. I'll have sandwich makings."

The laughter left her eyes. "You may not be here for Christmas."

"Yeah, I intend to… Oh, I get what you mean."

She sat with eyes downcast, chewing slowly. He studied her a moment before returning to his meal.

When she set her plate aside and touched her napkin to her lips, he stood with his own empty plate. "Ready for me to warm the pie? I have coffee making."

"I can warm it. You don't have to keep doing things for me." She stood and reached for his empty plate.

"I like working in the kitchen." He waited with an outstretched hand for her to hand him her plate. She seemed a little dubious but handed it over. He grinned at her. "You don't believe me." Was she always so quick to mistrust a person's words and intentions, or was it just him?

After he'd gone, she went to the hearth and used the blackened poker to move burning logs around in the fireplace. She was lifting another stick of firewood when he stuck his head around the door. "Do you want…? Here, let me do that!"

She shot him a hostile look and swung away from his outstretched hands with the wood in her arms.

He backed away, hands raised in surrender. "Sorry, I forgot for a moment. You're not a weak, helpless female."

After placing the stick of wood in the fireplace behind a smaller, fast-burning one, she brushed her hands together to remove clinging specks of bark. "Are you used to being around weak and helpless females?"

"Only when I try to help them overcome being weak and helpless."

"What were you about to ask me?"

"If you want a scoop of ice cream on your pie."

"Just pie and coffee, please."

He brought a coffeepot and two dessert plates in on a tray and set them on the hearth. He grinned at her. "Do you want to pour your own coffee or do you trust me to pour it?"

She returned his grin with a chuckle. "You can pour it. Just don't pour while holding the cup over my lap. I don't trust you not to spill it."

He laughed as he handed her a piece of pie. But he held the cups over the tray to pour their coffee. "Do you want to look through decorations this evening? I brought them inside." He sat in the armchair and crossed his legs, a foot propped on a knee.

"No. I can't stay that late. I have to get up early for work."

Besides, she needed to think awhile about whether she wanted to share such a family-type activity with him, when he might have a family someplace else. She felt a little uncomfortable even being here with him when he might be married. But looking at him in the firelight, as he munched pie and stared into the flames, she told herself there was no need to even think about that. Any wife should know she didn't have to worry about someone like Kate when a man as handsome and nice as he was could have any woman in the world.

Setting aside her empty pie plate and cup, she stood. "I'd better go." She went to the coatrack beside the door and lifted down her jacket.

A big hand took it from her. Steve held the coat for her to put her arms into the sleeves. He reached round her and pulled it together.

She felt his breath stir her hair and gulped as she reached for the zipper.

He held the opening together while she zipped it, and then he gave her shoulders a quick squeeze. "Are you coming back Saturday afternoon to help me with a tree?"

She looked at him over her shoulder. "Of course I'm coming. I can't have you cutting every tree on the place, trying to find just the right one." She reached for the doorknob.

"Wait!" His hand covered hers. "I have something for you."

He hurried to the desk and took a small object from a drawer. He came back, pressed it against her palm and closed her fingers around it.

She opened her hand and stared. *A key.*

"You might want to come by sometime while I'm gone. I go into Birmingham a couple of days a week to—work in an office. Usually Tuesdays and Thursdays."

Stunned by the key, Kate was halfway home before she thought to wonder what kind of office he worked in. And what did he mean when he said he tried to help women overcome being weak and helpless?

Chapter 10

Kate held her breath as Paul Jr. walked to the free-throw line.

Placing the toes of his sneakers at the line, he glanced over his shoulder at the bleachers.

Kate held up a thumb and forefinger, forming the letter *O*. She mouthed, *Okay*.

Paul Jr. nodded. A smile spread across his face. He turned and aimed.

Kate held her breath again as the ball ran around the rim. Then she jumped to her feet. "It went in! It went in! Way to go, Pauley."

She clapped and cheered with the crowd as they gave Paul Jr.'s winning shot a standing ovation.

Boys in gym shorts swarmed the court. The crowd roared as two players hoisted Paul Jr. onto their shoulders. Smiling, he waved proudly while his teammates carried him around the court.

Afterward, he insisted Kate go with him, his coach,

team members and team parents to celebrate with burgers and cokes. He introduced her as "my good friend Kate."

She sat crammed into a booth with several of the boys while they ate burgers.

"You oughta taste the chocolate cakes Kate bakes." Pauley's cheeks puffed out full of burger as he spoke.

The boy called Skeeter rubbed his stomach. "Yum, my favorite."

"Maybe she'll make one and let me bring a piece to school to share sometime." Pauley slanted a look at Kate. "Reckon you could, Kate?"

Kate smiled. "I'll sure try." She would love adding a little more joy to the boy's life. Of course, she would have to get his father's okay first.

Kate left the group in the McDonald's parking lot with boys and parents calling goodbye and inviting her back for their next game. She hummed a peppy little tune as she drove toward the old house, sun shining through her windshield.

Then her cell phone rang.

Steve hurried to stay in step with Kate as she kicked her way through fallen leaves.

"I don't know what made Mother decide to come take me shopping. She knows we never agree on what I wear. She always picks something skimpy or slinky that would never look good on someone as big as me."

Steve stopped walking, cocked his head to one side, grinning at her.

She stopped, too. "What?"

"You're not so big."

"Next to you, I'm not. But beside my sister and cousins, even my mother, I am." She started walking again.

He switched the ax from his right shoulder to his left and grabbed her arm. "Slow down, Kate. We have plenty of time. If your mom was just leaving Huntsville when she called, we don't have to be in a rush to get the tree. We can trim it later."

She stopped walking and looked at him. Their warm breath came out like little puffs of smoke in the frigid air.

"Look around you. What do you see?"

She glanced around them and shrugged. "Trees."

"Remember how you love trees? Remember how you love listening to the birds? And watching squirrels play?" He dropped her arm to gesture around them. "And look at this glorious sunshine. It came out today just for us. So we could go searching for a Christmas tree."

She gave him a weak smile. "You're right. I don't know why I let her get me so worked up. But now I'll have to leave early to wash my hair so I can go shopping with her. I guess you'll have to trim the tree without me."

"We can do it later."

She pulled a hank of hair around to examine it. "I'm thinking about cutting it. It takes too long to wash and dry it."

Cut? She would cut off that beautiful red-and-gold mane?

She lifted a handful of hair and let it fall a few strands at a time. It sparkled like flames in the sunlight. "And it's dead on the ends."

"Looks alive to me." He slipped off a glove and reached out playfully to touch it.

She caught her breath and looked at him.

And before he realized what he was doing, he had slid his hand beneath that glorious mop of curls to caress her cheek.

She didn't resist, just waited. The little puffs of warm air passing between her parted lips came out more quickly as green-and-gold-specked eyes searched his face.

He wanted to answer her silent question with a kiss.

But too many other questions needed to be answered first.

He took his hand away and pulled on his glove. "Let's go get that tree. I know where to find just the right one."

Kate followed him on wobbly legs. She had thought for a moment he was about to kiss her. Touching gloved hands to her warm cheeks, she pushed aside her disappointment. Her skin tingled where his hand had touched it. Why had he caressed her cheek, then withdrew his hand when he saw she was expecting a kiss?

She stumbled on a tree root, and he looked back at her. "You okay?"

Did he mean because she'd stumbled or because he'd started to kiss her and stopped?

"I'm fine." The words came out sharper than she intended. Because she was embarrassed or because she was angry with him?

Steve stopped, and she bumped into him.

"Sorry." He reached out as though to touch her, paused and pointed instead. "There it is. What do you think?"

Her gaze followed the path of his pointing finger. "Ohhh!" The involuntary exclamation puffed between her lips in a small white cloud.

A perfectly shaped cedar stood majestically alone atop a hillock. A clear blue winter sky spread above it. Its green boughs sparkled in the sun.

She stared in awe. "It's perfect! If we could take the sunlight home with us, we wouldn't need artificial lights."

Steve took another whack at the tree trunk. It was larger than he'd first thought.

"Maybe you should've brought the chainsaw," Kate called.

"Nah. Need to chop down an old-fashioned Christmas tree the old-fashioned way." He raised his arms, took a deep breath and let the ax fall. "Especially when it's going to stand in an old-fashioned parlor."

As soon as he said it, he knew he'd said the wrong thing. He glanced at Kate and saw the closed look on her face. Memories had come between them again. She resented his being here in her family place.

But when the tree came down, she cheered and ran to help him drag it to the house. He smiled at her as they rested it against the edge of the front porch. "I'll stir up the fire if you'll put on the kettle for hot chocolate. Then I'll trim off some bottom limbs and find something for a holder."

"Thanks, but I'd better not wait for hot chocolate. I have to get ready to go shopping with Mother. A wasted afternoon."

"Cheer up, Katie. Try to have a good time with her today. And try to use a little tact with her." He grinned at her. "Don't be quite as blunt as you are with me."

She wrinkled her nose at him. "When are we going to decorate the tree?" She looked at him with a wistful expression. "You won't do it while I'm gone?"

"I told you it wouldn't be fun by myself. I'll be patiently waiting." *For more than your help with the tree.* He was surprised at the errant thought, and wondered at the questioning look she gave him. Had he said it aloud?

And what did the thought mean?

He thought of his failure to kiss her when she'd looked at him so expectantly in the woods. He'd told himself it was because he needed to go easy for her sake. He now admitted he needed to back off some for his own.

I meant I'll be waiting patiently for her to accept that the place now belongs to me, not to her. Nothing more. Maybe if he kept telling himself this he would come to believe it.

But it was hard for him to keep his resolve when those big green-gold eyes gave him such an imploring look.

"How about if we decorate tonight?" he said. "If you get through visiting with your mother in time. Afterwards, we can grab a bite to eat at a drive-through and ride around and look at the Christmas lights. How long has it been since you saw the nighttime view from Red Mountain?"

When her mother's white Mercedes turned into the driveway, Kate slung the strap of her bag over her shoulder and grabbed her tan jacket from a chair. She met her mother halfway to the car.

"My, my, to what do I owe this jubilant welcome? It's good to see you, too, Kate." Her mother reached out to hug her.

Kate returned the embrace, feeling guilty about her attitude toward her mother's visit. She really did seem glad to see her. Maybe the afternoon wouldn't be so bad after all. She hugged her a little tighter.

Her mother broke the embrace, stepped back and scrutinized her. "Surely you're not planning to wear *that*. I expected you to be ready when I got here."

"I *am* ready." Her shirt was new, her jeans clean. Steve's words came back to her. *Try to use a little tact with her.* She forced a smile. "I thought you might want to get through shopping so you can be back home before it gets so late."

"You're already trying to rush me off home? And I thought you ran out because you were happy to see me."

And just how happy were you to see me, Mother, when you saw how I'm dressed?

Her mother headed for the house. "You can change while I freshen up."

Kate sighed and followed her. *Sounds like we're in for a fun day.*

* * *

Neither spoke as they climbed into the Mercedes and fastened their seat belts. They were passing the road leading to the old farmhouse when Kate ventured to ask, "What do you suppose will happen to the farmhouse, now that Grandpa's gone?"

Her mother stared straight ahead. "That's not your concern."

You may not be concerned about it, Mother, but I care what happens to all our old family stuff. "Don't you care about the personal things?"

"Father didn't have all that much to care about. You knew your grandfather. Nice things didn't mean anything to him."

"Yes, but…"

"Don't try to start something and cause trouble in the family, Kate. Your uncles and I will take care of Father's affairs. It's not your place."

"Yes, Mother."

Kate crossed her arms over her midsection and stared out the window. So, she didn't intend to tell Kate about Grandpa's will and the sale of his land. She guessed that left things in her hands.

Her mother's voice broke into her thoughts. "I think we should start by getting your hair cut. There's a good salon at the Galleria."

Kate looked at her. "I think I'm old enough to decide when I want to cut my hair, Mother. Besides, I thought we were going to one of the shops here in town."

"You know there are no decent dress shops here. It doesn't take long to drive in to Hoover."

"All right, Mother. The Galleria. But no haircut today. I have other things to do this evening."

"This evening? Kate, there'll come a day when you'll wish you could spend time with your mother."

Alarm shot through Kate. "Mother! Are you sick?"

"Do I look sick?"

"No. But you sounded so…" Kate hushed. She'd do better keeping her mouth closed. Everything she said only made things worse.

Her mother slid a music CD into the player. The voice of a contemporary Christian singer filled the car.

Kate closed her eyes while praise music flowed about her. Maybe she really should work on her attitude toward her mother. *Lord, help me to be kind and more patient with my mother today. Help me be the woman Steve thinks I can be.*

Chapter 11

Kate hurried through the crowd moving toward Penny's at one end of the mall.

Her mother grabbed her arm. "Kate, wait. Slow down. You're running my legs off. I want to go in the men's shop over there. Your father needs a new white dress shirt."

Kate dodged between a woman pushing a stroller and a group of teenagers goofing off and entered the men's store. She headed toward stacks of white shirts near the back.

But she stopped short beside a rack of ties. Her eyes were drawn to one exactly the same shade of blue as Steve's eyes.

She fingered the rich fabric of the tie, wondering what he would look like in dress clothes. He had asked her out to eat fast food tonight. But with all the Christmas events coming up, maybe…

"If you're looking for a tie for your father, that won't work with his new suit."

"Just looking, Mother. But I think I will buy one as a

Christmas gift for him. Maybe this brown-and-beige one. It would match his brown suit."

"No. Move over and let me see." Her mother nudged her.

Kate sighed, stepped back and watched her mother finger the ties.

"This yellow one. The brown-and-beige one is too dull." She pulled the tie from the rack and handed it to Kate. "Now come help me find a shirt. Then we'll go find you a dress."

Kate stared in disbelief at the dress her mother pulled from a rack of dresses. It was way too sleazy, and it would cling.

"With a girdle to hold your stomach in, I think this might work." Her mother held the clothes hanger out to her.

"Girdle?"

"Keep your voice down, Kate." She shook the garment at Kate. Bright green silk shimmered in the overhead lights.

Be tactful with your mother.

Forget that, Steve, if it means wearing a girdle. "Women don't wear girdles nowadays, Mother."

"Of course they do, Kate. If they want to look nice in their clothing. Especially hefty ones."

Hefty?

Kate shook her head in exasperation and reached for the rack. She would try on the dress, but she would not wear a girdle. She refused to even look at the undergarment her mother extended toward her. It would take forever for her to wiggle into that thing, and they were already wasting a lot of valuable time messing around with clothes she didn't intend to wear.

She stepped into the dressing room and turned her back to the mirror. She peeled off her slacks and blouse and slid the green silk over her head. A hook in the back hung in her hair.

"Kate, how does it look?"

"Don't know yet, Mother." Kate fidgeted with the hook.

"Do you need help?"

"No, Mother. I'm… Ouch!" A couple of hairs came out with the hook.

"Are you all right?"

"I'm fine, Mother. I'll be out in a minute."

She pulled up the zipper in the back of the dress and turned toward the mirror.

And gaped. Was that her?

She closed her mouth and turned for a side view. She didn't need a girdle.

She turned to view her backside. Yes, she'd definitely lost a few pounds.

She turned for a front view again. "Just look at that."

"What did you say, Kate?"

"Nothing, Mother. I'll be right out."

She smoothed the silk over her hips. What would Steve think if he saw her in this dress?

"Kate. Let me see how it looks."

"Okay." Kate stepped from the dressing room. She wanted to throw her hands out to each side of herself and sing out, *Ta-dah*. But she was silent, waiting for her mother's reaction.

Her mother stood with a finger to her chin. Finally, she nodded. "Yes, I think that will do. I believe you've lost a little weight, Kate."

Why, thank you, Mother. You almost gave me a compliment. Kate turned back toward the dressing room door. Now she could grab a pair of shoes someplace and they'd go.

"Try this sweater and slacks." Her mother held two hangers.

"I don't need—"

"Try them." She shoved the hangers at Kate.

"Yes, Mother." She didn't bother to try to hide her irritation, but took the outfit inside the dressing room and closed the door.

She pulled on the pants and slid the sweater over her head, then glanced in the mirror. Yes, they would do. So she would take them, too. Anything to pacify her mother.

When Kate saw the total cost of the dress, pants and sweater on the charge slip her mother signed, she almost choked. Entering the shoe department, she whispered, "I'll pay for the shoes. You've spent so much already."

"Nonsense. This is your Christmas present. It will come out of your father's bonus. He made a bundle for the company this year with that new computer program."

"Okay. Thanks." Kate picked up a dressy flat on the display table.

Her mother took the shoe from her hand and set it back in place. "We want something more elegant."

Before today, Kate might have said, "Nothing elegant for this elephant." But, envisioning herself in the green dress, she nodded and followed her mother to a display of high-heeled dress shoes.

As they walked from the store a short while later, she felt like singing with the carolers she heard in the distance. She had lost noticeable weight. A bag containing a lovely silk dress hung across her arm, and a bag in her hand held elegant black pumps, along with a light foundation makeup that a salesclerk had shown her how to apply. The clerk had bolstered her spirits even more when she'd said, "You don't want anything heavy enough to cover those lovely freckles across your nose and cheeks."

Kate held her head a little higher as she followed her mother through the mall.

A tinkling sound met them as they entered the nine-story glass atrium. A carousel had been set up where the water fountain usually stood. Round-eyed children, some accompanied by adults, rode up and down, round and round on brightly painted pretend animals.

Kate glanced up at what was billed as the world's largest skylight. It looked as if it would still be early enough for Steve and her to decorate the tree and go for a drive. She turned to her mother. "What time do you have?"

Her mother huffed. "Oh, yes, I almost forgot you have something more important to do this evening."

"Never mind, Mother. Let's go listen to the singing at the other end of the mall."

Young children in white robes stood on a portable platform, singing her family's all-time favorite: "'Away in a manger, no crib for a bed…'"

Her mother leaned over and whispered, "You sang this in a church pageant when you were four, dressed in a white robe and holding a doll."

Kate was sure she saw tears in her eyes as she turned back toward the platform. Was her mother actually thinking of her with such tenderness? Tears came, too, to Kate's eyes as she watched her listen to the children. *I'll never speak harshly to her again.*

But during their drive home, Kate's mother continued to harp on Kate's hair and even suggested she do away with all her "ratty" blue jeans and T-shirts. And drop her horticulture classes. "You can get a degree in business without the dirty work, Kate. And now, with your grandfather gone…"

"With Grandfather gone…?" Kate stared at her. This was the last straw. "You don't want me *playing* in the dirt. So now he's gone, maybe I won't? Is that why you won't talk to me about Grandpa's place? You don't want a daughter of yours playing in the dirt?"

"Don't blame me, Kate," her mother said quickly. "I don't know why your grandfather did what he did, but…"

"What Grandfather did…? It wasn't Grandpa who sold his home, Mother."

"His home? That dilapidated old house? Why, he hadn't lived in it for years. It and everything in it was—"

"Just drop it, Mother. I don't want to hear it. Besides, you let me know on the way up here that you didn't want to talk to me about Grandpa's affairs."

Kate sank back in the seat and closed her eyes. It was a great close to a beautiful day. She bit her lip, determined not to cry in front of her mother.

A short while later, her mother pulled into the driveway at Rob and Ellendor's house. She killed the engine and turned to Kate. "Just go on with your plans for the evening, Kate," she snapped. "I see Ellendor and Rob's car is here. I'll visit with them awhile and go home." She stepped from the car and took a bag from the backseat.

Kate climbed out, gathered her own bags and turned to her mother. "I don't want us to part like this, Mother. I…"

Her mother nodded curtly and turned toward the house.

"Thank you, Mother, for the beautiful clothes."

If she heard Kate, she didn't reply.

Kate dragged along behind her with arms full of boxes and bags. She didn't know if she could stand to be with Steve this evening, either. She didn't think her emotions could withstand the wear and tear of being with him right now.

After she put the new clothes away, she took a deep breath. She knew she'd keep her word and go over to the old farmhouse. But Steve was turning out to be as unpredictable as her mother. She'd need to keep her wits about her.

Chapter 12

"If this is too difficult for you, we won't do it," Steve said gently.

Kate looked up from the old trunk, where she knelt lifting out Christmas ornaments.

Steve was leaning against the mantel watching her.

"I have to face it sometime." Sometime soon she would have to face that cold mound in the graveyard, too. Maybe when the ground thawed…

She forced a smile. "This couldn't be any more difficult than that shopping trip today."

"Really rough, huh?"

"No harder than usual, I guess. One minute Mother and I are at each other's throats and the next…" She paused, recalling the tears in her mother's eyes as they watched the children sing. "And the next we're sharing a tender moment."

"Like we do?"

The soft response snatched her attention back to the man

standing beside the mantel. "Sort of, I guess." She stood holding a plastic bag of multicolored lights. "So I guess it must be more my fault than hers, huh?"

"I'll call a truce if you will. Deal?"

She bit her lip as she stared at the hand he extended toward her. When she looked up into his face, the intensity of his gaze took her breath away. She turned away from him. "I'll think about it."

She was still confused over that near-kiss this afternoon. She wasn't ready for close contact with him again so soon. Not even to shake his hand.

She felt the heat of his gaze on her back as she fiddled with the string of lights. She turned and held them out to him. "Here, these will have to be untangled. Do you think you can handle that?"

"If I can't I'll call on my strong boss-woman." He took the lights and grinned at her.

She grinned back, and the tension was broken.

Steve stretched the electrical cord with the lights attached across the floor and down the small hallway, untangling them as he went. "I'll plug them in and see if they work."

Kate piled ornaments onto the sofa. "If some of them are burned out, I think I saw replacements in the trunk. Most of these ornaments are fine. A few are broken, but there are still plenty for our tree."

He grinned. *Our tree.* But he didn't comment. He didn't want to cause her to crawl behind her wall again.

She seemed fine now. The tense moment when she'd refused to shake hands had passed. At least she hadn't verbally attacked him again.

He didn't know what he was offering, anyway, when he offered to call a truce. Or what he was expecting from her.

How could he expect them to spend time together without crossing swords when so much stood between them?

She smiled and held out a tiny angel doll. "I'll hold the ladder if you'll do the honors." She glanced at the bare treetop.

He situated the angel at the top of the tree, and then backed down the ladder while Kate held it. When he stepped onto the bottom rung, he stood within the circle of her arms. With a sharp intake of breath, she removed her hands and turned away, her back straight and rigid.

If he took her in his arms now, she would respond to his embrace. But his better judgment overcame his desire and he turned away.

He cleared his throat before he spoke. "The lights should probably go on next."

"You're right." She bent and picked up the end of the light cord.

They worked for a few minutes without speaking. Then he turned the lights on.

Kate clapped in delight. "They're perfect. We don't need to move any of them around." She turned to the pile of ornaments on the sofa. "Now let's hang the ornaments. I picked out one that I want to place first in memory of Grandpa." She held up a gold-colored ornament in the shape of a star.

Steve smiled. Maybe they were about to work through some of the barriers.

When they finished decorating the tree, they hung a Christmas wreath on the front door and placed red candles in crystal holders on the mantel. Around the candleholders, they arranged the branches Steve had trimmed from the bottom of the tree.

Standing back to admire their handiwork, Kate looked at him and smiled. "I didn't realize you had such an artist's eye."

He grinned. "Maybe being around you made it rub off on me."

"Maybe." She gave him a smug look and then wrinkled her nose at him.

Without realizing he was about to do it, he placed an arm around her shoulders and squeezed them. But he quickly dropped his arm and turned away. "We better get a move on if we're going to take a drive and grab a bite to eat."

Kate wiped the mustard from her chin with a paper napkin and smiled across the pickup console at Steve. "Thank you, kind sir. That was great."

Steve returned the smile. "You're welcome, my fair lady. Hot dogs are one of my favorite meals."

Kate sat forward on the pickup seat and peered through the windshield, letting her gaze roam the valley below them. "I can't get over how many lights there are now across the city. I know lots of them are Christmas lights. But they're spread out almost as far as the eye can see."

"Just wait until you see them from the top of Vulcan."

"Vulcan? I haven't been there in years. Since before he was taken down for repairs—about 1999, I think. Do you remember when he used to hold a torch with a light in it? The light was normally green, and then when there was a traffic death in Birmingham, it turned red. They didn't put it back in his hand after repairing him, though."

"But they do still have it," Steve said. "It's in the museum there in the statue's pedestal. Visitors to the museum can touch a button to make it light up. I brought a group of kids up here once who were fascinated with it."

"Do you think the museum and the new viewing platform will be open tonight?"

He grinned. "Every night till ten, the internet said."

"Great. Let's go."

* * *

Standing in the parking lot at Vulcan Park, Kate gazed up at the 56-foot iron man standing atop a 124-foot tower. "It never ceases to amaze me how such a big hunk of metal could be moved from location to location as this one was for over thirty years. Then be hoisted above such a high tower here on top of the mountain."

"What I think about when I look at him is how much we humans are like him."

"How is that?"

"He stands there atop the mountain like he owns it when, in fact, he came from the very dirt on which he stands."

"Oh?"

"He's made of red iron ore that was mined from this mountain."

"This very mountain we're standing on? I never realized that." She looked up at the statue and shook her head. "Amazing."

He nodded his head in agreement. "It amazes me, too, that a pagan Roman god is the center of so much attention right in the middle of the Bible Belt."

"Vulcan, god of the forge. He's standing on a mountain of red iron ore, overlooking what was once known as a steel town."

"Good explanation." He grabbed her hand. "Come on. We don't want to be standing out here in the parking lot when the observation tower closes."

She let him lead her toward the entranceway.

But just before they got too close to the base to see the top, she looked up again and shook her head. "Just a pile of dirt."

Kate thought about Steve's words as they rode up in the glass-enclosed elevator. *He stands there atop the mountain like he owns it, when he came from the very dirt on which he stands.*

The words reminded her of a familiar Bible verse: *For dust thou art, and unto dust shalt thou return.* As Steve stood looking through the glass at the lights flashing by them, she quietly considered the verse. *So, we came from the dust just as the iron man did. But we can take none of it with us when we leave this world. Grandpa couldn't take the land he loved with him and it was left for people to squabble over. It was here way before we were, and really doesn't belong to any of us.*

"Look, Katie, spread out before us."

Steve's voice jarred her from her reverie, drawing her attention to the view outside their glass enclosure as it moved upward. A sea of lights—stars above, city lights below—twinkled beyond the glass. Now, *there* was the amazing sight.

The elevator stopped and the doors opened. A girl and boy, who looked to be in their midteens, waited outside the doors, arms entwined.

Kate glanced at Steve. When he smiled down at her she smiled back, determined to push thoughts of the land fight from her mind for the time being. She would not let anything mar this beautiful night.

Steve stepped out of the elevator onto the glass-enclosed observation deck. When he felt Kate hesitate, he gave her hand a little tug. "Come on. The glass protects us. We can't fall off."

"That's what I thought when I climbed the tree that day. When you tried to catch me in a wheelbarrow." She gave him a mock dirty look as she stepped out of the elevator.

Chuckling, he slipped an arm around her shoulders. "Come this way. I want you to see the view from over here."

He led her to a secluded spot overlooking the city's Southside. He heard a soft "wow" escape Kate's lips, just before she looked up at him with eyes outshining the stars and the city lights. "It's like a fairy la—"

Her words trailed off as her eyes met his. Her lips were too close to ignore. He lowered his face toward hers, and she hesitated only a moment before melting into his embrace.

Steve's heart gave a jolt as her lips met his. He pulled her even closer.

Remember all the questions between you.

He tore his lips away and released her.

Kate stepped back, swaying toward the glass. He reached out to grab her arm to keep her from falling, but she steadied herself and turned away from him.

There I go, disorienting her like I did in the woods this morning. Was she angry with him again? He'd have to be more careful to keep his emotions under control when he was with her. At least until they got this land thing settled.

"What's that building over there to the right?" She pointed with a finger against the glass.

He moved to her side, careful not to touch her, and looked where she pointed.

They stood for a while, peering out over the city, picking out familiar landmarks and recalling what once stood where. Kate remembered driving her grandpa up here to take care of insurance business at the Liberty National building, which had a small replica of the Statue of Liberty mounted atop it.

"And we shopped at the big Sears store that sat over there on First Avenue. Oh, and the most heavenly smell of freshly baked bread enveloped the area every time you drove through." Closing her eyes, she sucked in a deep breath of air as though she could still smell the bread.

She opened her eyes. "It came from a factory where they made bread. Merita Bread, I think."

"I remember it. We used to come to Birmingham quite often."

They pointed out a few more landmarks and commented on them before Steve checked his watch. "Ready to go back down? We need a little time to look at things in the museum before it closes for the night."

There were few other visitors in the museum at this late hour. So they moved quickly about, viewing the exhibits and reading the history of Vulcan.

Steve stopped at the torch Vulcan had once held in his hand. "Do you want to push the button and see it light up?"

"Sure." They watched the light turn green, then red, the way it once did when there was a traffic fatality in the city. Kate thought of the time she drove Grandpa into Birmingham to see a doctor and they were held up by a gruesome accident where two teenagers were killed. The light was red as they drove back out of town. She shuddered and moved on.

As they stepped from the building, she glanced at Steve in the glow of the lights illuminating the statue. "That was fun."

His warm fingers wrapped around hers as they walked toward his pickup. He smiled at her and she was reminded of his kiss on the observation platform.

Why had she moved away from him so quickly afterward? Sure, the kiss had done something strange to her insides, something that made her dizzy. Sure, she'd almost toppled through the window to the ground 120 feet below. But she could have grabbed him for support.

Taking care of her grandfather, she'd had little time for romance in high school—even if a boy had been interested in her. She recalled being kissed only three times before tonight. Once, when the teacher left the room during eighth-grade social studies class, Jimmy Cole and Jerry Brooks went around the room taking turns holding all the girls for each of them to kiss. Some of the girls giggled and kissed the boys back. Others, like Kate, tried to fight them off and were too embarrassed to report what happened.

As she grew older, Kate wasn't averse to being kissed, but the right opportunity had just never presented itself until she was a sophomore at the university. Melvin Pickwell had walked her to the dorm after an evening business class and asked if he could kiss her good-night. She consented out of curiosity and wondered afterward, *So what's all the fuss about a kiss?*

And now she knew. A delicious shiver ran through her.

"Cold?" He dropped her hand and placed an arm around her shoulders.

"Only a little." She felt plenty warm just remembering his kiss. But if she told him she wasn't cold, he might take his arm away.

After he opened the truck door for her, he pulled a blanket from the second seat and tucked it around her. "You should be toasty warm in no time. The pickup has a good heater."

Kate smiled as she snuggled under the blanket. She wouldn't worry tonight about how she felt about Steve. Or how he felt about her. She'd just enjoy this magic night and their ride home together.

And she wouldn't worry about her family's land.

After all, as Scarlett O'Hara said, *Tomorrow is another day.* She'd sort it out later.

Kate's and Steve's conversation was light and impersonal as they drove home. They admired the elaborate Christmas creations decorating old mansions and expansive lawns in an older section of Homewood. They exclaimed again over the lights of the city from an overlook on Double Oak Mountain.

When they reached Steve's front yard, he jumped out of the truck as soon as it stopped.

Kate waited while he ran around and opened her door. "I wish you had let me come pick you up so you wouldn't have to drive home this late alone, Katie."

"It's only about a quarter of a mile down the road. Besides, I'm a big girl now."

He laughed. "Of course you are. But my mama taught me to be a gentleman. Or at least she tried."

Kate smiled up at him as they crossed the yard in the moonlight. "Oh, I don't think she did such a bad job. And I thank you, kind gentleman, for a great time this eve…" Her foot slipped on gravel and she stumbled.

Steve caught her in his arms. He looked down at her in surprise, touched his lips lightly to hers and then put her away from him. "Good night, Kate." He spoke softly as he opened her car door. "Sleep tight."

She slid onto the car seat, too flustered to explain to him how she'd wound up in his arms.

"I know he thought I was looking for a good-night kiss," she muttered, gunning the motor as she started up the driveway. Her face burned as she thought about the way he only briefly touched his lips to hers before pulling away. Evidently their earlier kiss had not meant to him what it had to her.

Well, she would just put that kiss and their entire evening together out of her mind. Like she hoped to soon put Stephen Q. Adams out of her house.

Chapter 13

A few days before Christmas, Kate stood at the printer watching it spit out the pages of a legal document.

A sudden gust of wind swept in as the back door burst open. "Where's Daddy?" Paul's daughter burst in. "Is Daddy here?" Her voice held a note of desperation and she looked frantically around the outer office. "I didn't see his car."

"It's being serviced. He's in his office. Are you all right, Lisa?"

The girl ran back outside without answering.

Kate reached the open doorway as a car drove away.

Lisa ran back in, almost knocking her down. "I need Daddy."

"I'll let him know."

Mr. Boyer walked out of his office, papers in his hand. "Lisa! What are you doing here?"

Lisa let out a wail. "Mommy's not coming home today like she said." She ran to clasp him around the waist.

"How do you know she's not coming today?"

Kate closed the door and walked back to the printer.

Lisa looked up at her father with tears in her eyes. "She called Mrs. Mason. She was supposed to meet me here. She promised to take me shopping for a new outfit for Julie's party."

Kate watched printed sheets slip into the printer tray.

Her boss untangled himself from his daughter's arms, handed Kate the papers he was holding and then looked at his daughter. "Why are you here so early? Are you skipping school? Who brought you?"

"Don't you remember, Daddy? Today's the beginning of Christmas vacation. I told you we were getting out of school at lunchtime." She let out an anguished cry and clasped him round the waist again. "And Mommy's not here like she promised." Tears streamed down her face.

He glanced at Kate. "Calm down, Lisa. You're embarrassing Miss Sanderson." He took Lisa's shoulders and turned her toward his office. "I'm sure your mother will be home by the weekend."

"But that's too late." Lisa wailed her frustration and disappointment again. "Julie's party is tomorrow night. And I'm supposed to get my hair trimmed today, too."

He reached around her to push his office door open.

She looked up at him, a pleading expression on her pixie face. "Will you take me?"

"Lisa, I can't spend the afternoon in the mall. Mrs. Mason will take you. That's what I pay her for." He left Lisa and hurried to the back door. "Where is she?"

"She left me here. She has a doctor's appointment. Mommy was supposed to take me." She dropped her head and bit her lip. "I told her to go on, that I talked to you and you would take me."

"You shouldn't have told her such a thing." He looked at Kate.

She busied herself with papers from the printer.

He cleared his throat. "Miss Sanderson—uh, do you think…?"

She looked up as he approached the desk.

His expression was much like that his daughter had worn when she pleaded with him. "Could you possibly take her?"

Kate glanced at the papers on her desk. "What about these?"

"Those can wait until tomorrow." He looked at the papers she had taken from the printer. "You've finished the most urgent ones."

Lisa's tears stopped. She watched them with interest.

"I'll pay you for your time and trouble."

Lisa's young mouth hardened. Her eyes narrowed.

Kate smiled at her. "You don't have to pay me. I think I'd enjoy a shopping spree with Lisa. And I may get my own hair trimmed while hers is being done."

"All right!" A big smile spread across Lisa's face. "Can we go to the Galleria? There's a salon where I got my hair cut one time. You'll like it. They do all the new funky dos."

Kate laughed. "I don't know about a—*funky* do for me."

"Don't you come back here with purple hair, young lady." Her father pulled a bill from his wallet and handed it to her, then handed another to Kate. "That should do for your haircuts. Shouldn't it?"

Kate glanced at what he'd handed her. *A hundred dollars?* "Y-yes, sir. But you don't have to pay for mine." She reached the bill out to him.

"No, keep it. You probably wouldn't spend as much on a cut if you weren't taking Lisa. I'm sure you could get a less expensive one here in town."

"Then I will."

He held out two twenties. "This should get lunch. Lisa will probably want pizza and a half-dozen Coke refills."

He pulled out a credit card. "She should be able to get

what she wants with this. Have the clerk call me and I'll okay your signature."

Kate stood with her mouth agape while he extracted another card from his wallet. He handed it to her. "Stop at the station on the corner and fill your gas tank. I'll call and let Pete know you're coming. It will probably be late when you and Lisa get back, so she can bring the cards to me."

He looked at his daughter. "And don't you lose them, Lisa Louise."

Kate didn't bother to argue anymore. He seemed accustomed to such actions.

But not with her! She wondered if Jane got this kind of treatment from him.

"Come on, Kate. I'm starving." Lisa stood at the door, stuffing her hundred-dollar bill into her shoulder bag.

"On my way." Kate pulled her own bag from a drawer.

Her boss followed her to the door. When she lifted her tan jacket from the coatrack, he took it and held it for her to slip into. "Buy yourself a nice coat with one of those cards."

Kate's arm missed the coat sleeve. "Oh, no. I couldn't do that."

"A bonus. You've earned it. Stepping in to help me out while Jane's been indisposed." She slipped into her jacket and he patted her shoulder in a fatherly gesture.

She followed Lisa out the door, her cheeks burning even in the cold December air.

It was dark when Kate pulled her little car into the Boyers' circular driveway later that evening.

Lisa unlocked her seat belt and turned and smiled at her. "Thanks, Kate. I had a fantastic time."

Kate stopped the car at the front steps and returned the smile. "I'm glad. It was fun for me, too. I love your new clothes and your new hairdo. You're going to be the prettiest girl at the party."

Lisa patted her new bob. "It is pretty, isn't it?" She turned her head to one side and studied Kate in the light from the porch. "You look pretty, too, with your hair short. But I couldn't *believe* you were having it *all* cut off."

Kate laughed. "Well, I thought if I was going to do it, I may as well go all the way."

Lisa giggled. "You did, too. But it looks sooo good. I *love* it."

"Thank you. Now you'd better run in. Don't forget to give your father the credit cards."

Kate smiled as she watched Lisa run up the wide steps and let herself in the double doors of the white Victorian-style house. Then she pulled down the sun visor and looked at her reflection in the mirror on the back of it. She smiled. *I think I'm going to like it, too. If I ever get used to it.*

She raised the sun visor and glanced over her shoulder at the large box on the backseat. Her new hairdo should go great with her new black coat, green silk dress and black pumps.

The only problem now was finding someplace to wear them. *Or someone to wear them for.*

Chapter 14

Steve stirred the pot of chili hanging on a hook in the fire-place. He straightened and listened again. Was that a car?

He went to the window and looked out. No car lights. She hadn't even been by to admire the Christmas tree.

He pulled the rocker close to the fire, sat down and propped his work boots on the hearth. He stared into the flames. Was she angry with him for kissing her? The look in her eyes on the balcony at Vulcan had appeared to give him consent. Of course, she could have just been caught up in the magic of the night. Like he was. Standing above the city lights, blanketed with a canopy of stars, who could help but feel romantic?

But in the front yard, when she'd stumbled and fallen into his arms, that was a different story. He was lucky she hadn't hauled off and walloped him.

He thought about the first time he saw her, when she'd come storming into camp and knocked him off his stool. Man, she was something with those green-and-gold-flecked eyes snapping and that red hair flaming around her face.

He probably should check on her.

He touched the phone on his belt. Why had he never thought to get her cell number? He should have the house number someplace.

He went to the desk, took an envelope from the drawer and pulled out several papers. He laid aside the deed Kate's mother and uncles had given him and picked up a sheet of handwritten notes. "Aha, here it is."

He punched in the number, but no one answered.

As he slid the envelope back inside the desk drawer, another document caught his attention. He pulled it out, unfolded it and frowned.

Every time he read this thing, he became more puzzled. For the life of him, he couldn't figure out the reasoning behind such action. Sooner or later, Kate was bound to find a record of this document—unless he could convince her to give up the search. And he could think of no way to do that short of handing the place over to her.

Even if he could afford to do such a thing, or had the inclination to do it, he couldn't just drop plans for the property. It would affect too many other lives. Young, innocent lives.

He slid the document under other papers and closed the drawer.

Standing with a hand propped against the mantel, he watched red-and-gold flames leap up the chimney. *The color of Kate's hair.*

If he didn't hear from her today, he'd go by the house in the morning on his way to Atlanta.

On Monday Kate hurried from the car to the back door of the law office, shivering in the cool morning air. She liked the way her short hair curved around her cheeks, but her ears and neck missed the warmth of her long mass of curls.

She hung her jacket on a hook inside the back door, opened her bag and dropped her keys inside. Smiling, she pulled out the slip of paper she'd found on Aunt El's front door when they'd returned from the grocery store Saturday.

She read it again.

Dear Kate. On my way to Atlanta for Christmas. Back around 3:00 p.m. Sunday. How about supper? I'll cook.

She hugged the note to her. Steve wanted to see her again.

"Excuse me. May I help you?"

Kate jumped and turned.

Mr. Boyer stood by the door with briefcase in hand. A shocked look crossed his face. "Miss Sanderson! I didn't recognize you."

Kate smiled and touched her hair. "Thank you for the haircut."

"You're welcome. It looks nice."

Kate felt herself blush. "Thank you."

He bustled toward his office door. "I hope you bought the coat, like I said."

"Y-yes, I did. It…"

But he had disappeared inside his office.

When he came out, she glanced at the plastic container sitting on the top of a file cabinet. "Would you like a slice of chocolate cake?"

His eyes widened. Then he smiled. "Yes. Thank you. That sounds good." He pulled a chair near her desk and sat down, waiting while she cut the cake and served him a slice on a small paper plate. After he took the first bite,

Kate almost laughed aloud at how much his expression was like his son's the day he'd shared her cake.

"Katerina—that is the correct pronunciation of your name, isn't it?" He took another bite.

Kate nodded.

"I've been thinking I should hire another full-time person for the office. Jane will likely be out a good deal with her baby. I was wondering if you might be interested."

Kate's mouth dropped open. "But I have another term at the university before I get my diploma."

"I understand. But, if you would like to train as a legal assistant, you can go to evening classes locally."

"Legal assistant? Me? I—don't know. I'll have to think about it."

"I—the firm, that is—would pick up the tab. A lot of employers today pay educational expenses for employees."

"Yes, someone told me McDonald's does that."

A wry smile twisted his lips. "I think your talents would be wasted slinging hamburgers." He took another bite of cake. "This is very good."

He licked icing from a finger, and then picked up the napkin Kate laid before him. "You can think about my offer and let me know." He cleaned his fingers on the napkin and threw it in the wastebasket. Then he picked up his chair and placed it against the wall before turning toward his office.

Legal assistant. Kate turned to the computer shaking her head. *I can't see me as a legal assistant.*

Well, right now she didn't have time to think about it. She had to get these letters typed or she wouldn't have a job at all.

She began keying in the first letter her boss had dictated but stopped and turned toward his office door when she failed to hear it close. He stood in the open doorway looking at her.

She frowned. "Did you need something else?"

He cleared his throat. "Uh, no. Not right now." He turned to step inside his office. But as she turned back to the computer, she heard him clear his throat again. "I would like for you to accompany me to court in the morning."

"Me?"

"To take notes. It's the Lockhart case you typed up notes for earlier. Print out a copy and study them. We'll go over them later."

"Y-yes, sir."

"I think tomorrow will wrap up the case and then we can close the office until after the holidays."

"Yes, sir."

"And you don't have to say 'sir' to me. I'm not all that old."

"No, sir. I mean, no, you aren't—old."

She stared at the closed door after he left the office. Why had his attitude toward her suddenly changed? He was calling her by her given name. And not just Kate, but Katerina, as though it fit her.

She glanced down at her black slacks and new white blouse with simulated pearl buttons at the wrist, which she had bought on her own credit card. She touched her hair. Was it her new look? Had a haircut, a little makeup and different clothing changed her so much in his estimation?

Maybe it was because she'd been nice to his children. And helped him with them. Or was it because she could bake cakes?

What kind of assistance would he expect from her if he paid for her to go to school?

Kate, stop being so cynical. And speak up about the legal help you need while you have a little leverage.

The next time he came through the office, on the way to the door with his briefcase, she cleared her throat and stood. "Mr. Boyer, I really do need to talk to you about my grandfather's—"

The telephone cut her words short. He waited while she answered it.

"Hi, Kate. How are you?"

"Hello, Lisa. I'm fine." She glanced at her boss. He made a move toward the desk. "Do you want to talk to your father?"

"No. I called to tell you about the great time I had at the party."

Kate shook her head at Mr. Boyer and pointed at herself.

He nodded, looking relieved, and hurried out the door.

She wondered if he was relieved because he didn't have to talk to his daughter or because he could postpone— again—talking to *her* about her grandfather's will.

Whatever it was, she couldn't worry about it now. She had to print out Mr. Boyer's notes on the Lockhart case and try to wrap her mind around it before court convened in the morning.

She also had to put together something to wear and see what she could do with her hair.

Lord, don't let me look like a redneck in court tomorrow. Or act like one.

"Don't you think so, Kate?"

Oops. She had forgotten she was supposed to be talking to Lisa on the telephone. She put the receiver closer to her ear. "I'm sorry, Lisa, I didn't hear what you said."

"I said, don't you think I look older with my hair shorter?"

"Uh, yes, Lisa, I think you probably do. But I hope I don't." Kate gave a short laugh. "Don't look older with my hair short, I mean."

Lisa giggled. "I knew what you meant. I don't know if you look older. But you sure do look pretty. I'll bet Daddy thinks you do, too."

Kate started. Maybe he did, the way he acted. Kate

wasn't sure she wanted him to think she was pretty, the way his attitude toward her had so suddenly changed.

She didn't know the man well enough to have an idea of what he was really like. She knew he was divorced and his wife seemed to feel she still had a claim on him, which he didn't seem to appreciate. Maybe he's the one who had initiated the divorce so he could be free to chase other women.

"Are you still there, Kate?"

"Uh, yes, Lisa. But I'm pretty busy. Why don't you call me later in the week and see if we can work out a time to get together again. Maybe have a soda or something."

"Super. How about Wednesday?"

"Check with me and we'll see."

They hung up and Kate's mind whirled. Could Mr. Boyer be interested in her? That would figure, when the man whose interest she actually wanted kept pushing her away.

Chapter 15

Kate hurried up the courthouse steps beside Paul Boyer, silently repeating the prayer she had already uttered half a dozen times that morning. *Lord, give me strength and courage to face this day. Help me do whatever it is I need to...*

"Paul Boyer!"

A nice-looking young man with a red tie flapping in the wind bounced down the steps toward them. He stopped and extended a hand to her boss.

Mr. Boyer introduced him as attorney Jeff Kanockus. And her as his new legal aide.

The young man enveloped Kate's hand in his and smiled into her eyes. "Lovely. I wouldn't mind her aiding me sometimes." He quirked an eyebrow at her boss as he captured his tie from the wind.

Mr. Boyer laughed lightly, looking pleased.

Kate slid her hand from the young man's grasp, trying to appear composed and professional, as if she was accustomed to such remarks.

She had dug through one of her unpacked bags and found a white pullover sweater and midcalf black skirt, which she folded over and pinned at the waist. Topped with a gray blazer her mother had bought her last Christmas, and which she had never worn, it worked. A red scarf around her neck added a touch of cheerfulness and helped compensate for the loss of warmth due to the haircut. Her new black coat and high-heeled pumps completed her outfit.

She had used Aunt El's styling iron to smooth her hair, which a hot shower had curled tightly around her head. It now looked almost as nice as when the stylist had fixed it.

"It was good meeting you, Katerina." The young attorney flashed her a bright smile. "I hope to see you again soon."

He nodded at the soft leather briefcase Mr. Boyer had insisted Kate carry, more for appearance than usefulness, she was sure. "Looks like you two have a busy day ahead of you, too."

Her boss nodded. "Yes, an important case to argue. I'm pleased to have Miss Sanderson on board."

Kate almost laughed aloud. Now she understood why he wanted her here. Her presence, with her new professional look, was also for appearances. She had a feeling this was going to be an interesting day.

Kate and her employer left the courtroom a few minutes before five that evening with other legal personnel and spectators. She was surprised to realize she was not nervous at all after court convened. She was too engrossed in the proceedings.

He beeped the remote to open the door to the Lexus, then opened Kate's door for her. "How about we have dinner to celebrate our win today?"

Kate smiled. *Our win?* He was acting as if she had had something to do with it.

"We can drive out to the new place on Lay Lake. It has the best steaks and catfish around."

"Sure." Kate slid onto the car seat. It was okay for a lawyer and his assistant to celebrate together after winning a big case, wasn't it?

She wondered if her sister celebrated with her handsome young assistant after a win.

When they pulled into a lit parking space at a low, lodge-like building beside the lake, Kate smiled at the man beside her. "It's beautiful."

Tall pines swayed in the breeze. Moonlight sparkled on the water of the Coosa River out back. Stepping from the car, Kate shivered in the sharp breeze off the water and pulled the red scarf more snugly about her neck.

Paul Boyer put an arm around her shoulders as though to warm her, and hurried her toward the building. "There will be roaring fires to warm us inside."

Stepping inside the double doors, she glanced around the long room. Candles cast a rosy glow around white-draped tables. Log fires burned in stone fireplaces at each end of the room. The place was toasty warm. Only about half the tables were occupied. Conversation was subdued and soft music played in the background.

Mr. Boyer helped her out of her coat and hung it and his top coat on wooden pegs by the door.

"Paul! It's good to see you." The smiling bleached-blonde hostess approached with menus in her hand. "Your favorite table should be empty in just a sec. Do y'all wanna sit by the fire while I get the table cleared for you? I can bring coffee. Do you want the usual?"

"Yes, the usual, Jo Dean. Steaks and shrimp. For both of us. And coffee by the fire sounds great."

Paul steered Kate to the fireplace nearest them, where they seated themselves in rockers. Paul extended well-manicured hands toward the flames. A diamond ring glittered on his finger. Every silky brown hair on his head was in place, even after he'd rushed through the wind. His dark coat and trousers were spotless, and the white shirt he'd worn all day still looked crisp.

Kate glanced down at herself and smiled. She still looked neat, too. Even her hands were neat now, no more broken and stained nails. The manicure she'd had with Lisa at the mall had worked wonders.

Paul looked at her and smiled. "Nice."

"Very." She had a strange feeling he wasn't speaking of only the fire and their surroundings.

He was a nice man, she assured herself. Smooth-looking, smooth-speaking. But nice. Settling back on the pillowed seat of the wooden rocker, she watched bright flames dart up the large rock chimney. She breathed in the mouth-watering aroma of char-grilled steak, which she would soon be eating on a white-draped table with candles.

But, to her, all this couldn't compare to the enjoyment of sitting in a rough, timeworn rocking chair beside a small and ancient rock fireplace, with a weather-beaten, bushy-headed and bushy-faced man in beat-up jeans and scuffed boots, eating homemade vegetable soup.

But she was here tonight. Her mirror, and the admiring eyes of other people today, told her she looked good. She had spent an interesting day watching intelligent people at work. And she had learned some things about the justice system in her country. She would enjoy the present.

She would forget about what happened in the past, and what might or might not happen in the future.

For tonight, anyhow.

After they were seated at their table and the server had brought their salads, Paul picked up his salad fork and looked at Kate. "I saw what you were sketching today."

Kate's face warmed. "I'm sorry. I know I was there to

take notes. But I couldn't resist sketching the defendant. He had such an unusual face."

"Not so unusual to me. He has the same sneaky expression as most of the common criminals who come through the courts."

Kate stared at him, a tiny tomato on her fork suspended before her open mouth. "Common criminal? If you think he's guilty, why did you defend him?"

"My job. He's entitled to defense."

"But you helped him go free. And all those other people congratulated you."

"They recognized a job well done, Katerina."

"Surely all of them don't think he's innocent, if his own lawyer doesn't."

"It's the way our justice system works." He took a swallow of tea. "Do you still want to be a part of the legal world?"

"I never said I did." She put the tomato in her mouth and chewed.

His face registered surprise.

Was he surprised because she'd hinted she might refuse his offer to work for him full-time and let him foot the bill for her training as a legal assistant? Or was he shocked she would speak to him the way she did?

She picked up her knife and cut a large piece of lettuce leaf. She was surprised at herself, too. What had given her the courage to speak to her boss as she had? Was it because he didn't seem like her boss tonight? Or because she had newfound confidence in herself?

"What did *you* think, Katerina? After reading all my notes from the previous day in court, then sitting in on the closing day of the trial?" He leaned across the table, watching her, as if he really cared what she thought.

And what did she think? Paul had presented such a

brilliant defense she hadn't thought to doubt the man's innocence.

"Did you think he was innocent when you read my notes and my interview with him?"

"Well, I…"

"See?" He sat back in his chair, smiling smugly. "Innocent until proven guilty." He forked a bite of salad into his mouth and chewed.

"Still…"

"I just presented the facts given to me and…"

"Did you do any investigating on your own?"

His smile turned to one of amusement. "See, you would make a great legal assistant. You would be careful to check all the facts. And you're becoming a pretty good interrogator."

She smiled at his obvious reference to the way she queried him.

But his tone turned serious. "Can you draw a person's face from someone's description?"

"I don't know. I've never tried. Why?"

"I think your sketching ability—if what I saw today is any indication—would come in handy in trying to identify suspects. If you can draw the face of someone you've never seen simply by hearing someone else describe it…"

Excitement began to tickle Kate's brain—and her stomach. This appealed to her artistic side. But could she do it? Did she want to?

The waitress set large platters of steak, shrimp and baked potatoes before them. Paul pointed at Kate's plate with his fork. "Don't worry about it right now. Your dinner will get cold. We'll discuss it more later."

She cut into her steak and took a bite. But the chef's talents and Paul's further attempts at conversation were wasted on her as she thought about the insinuation that his client was guilty, and his question about what *she* thought.

They were almost through with the meal when he regained her attention with another stab at humor. "Where are you tonight, Katerina?" He wore an amused smile. "Still trying to decide if the man's guilty?"

She started and shook her head to clear it. She felt herself blush. "Yes, I guess so. I was going over all he said in court today, and the way he said it, to see if I could detect a lie or deception in there someplace."

"And?" His smile mocked her.

She lifted her chin a bit and looked at him coolly. "And, I haven't decided for sure yet."

He gave a low chuckle. "Be sure to let me know when you do." The smile was still on his lips, but his gaze intensified as he looked at her.

He reached across the table and took her hand. "You're a lovely young woman, Katerina." He spoke softly, causing her cheeks to grow hot again. "You've been hiding your beauty under that screen of hair. And…" He paused and looked at her more sharply, as though testing the waters. "And under shapeless clothing."

Her cheeks grew even hotter. Flustered, she slid her hand from his and reached for her bag on the chair beside her. She pulled out her cell phone and checked the time. "It's getting late. We should go."

"We haven't had dessert." He held up a finger to summon their waitress. "You may bring our dessert now, Lucy. Bring us the cherry cheesecake."

Kate spoke up. "I think I'll have apple pie. Without ice cream." *I like my new figure and I want to keep it.*

She smiled at Paul's raised eyebrows. Was he surprised she didn't want cheesecake, or because she had usurped his authority?

Paul kept his hands and fresh remarks to himself while they ate their desserts and sipped decaf coffee. On the way back to the office parking lot where Kate left her car, she dozed in the warm interior of Paul's luxurious automobile.

"How about a nightcap at my place?"

"No, thank you."

"I left the coffee ready to drip. And we don't have to get up early. I thought I'd close the office until after Christmas."

"That sounds good, and it's been a great day. But a long one. I want to go home and sleep."

"Maybe another time?" When she didn't answer, he turned up the volume on the CD player and turned his attention to the road.

Words and music of an old love ballad surrounded them. "My heart is longing for you…"

Kate cushioned her head against the car seat and suppressed a sigh. Five more days until Steve would be back.

Chapter 16

On Christmas morning Kate dressed carefully in the new pants and sweater her mother had bought her on their shopping trip together. She opened the front door to her mother shortly before noon.

"Kate! I'm glad you took my advice and had your hair cut."

Kate took the casserole dish from her mother's hands. *I didn't take your advice, Mother. I'd already decided to cut it before you said anything.* "Where are Daddy and Billy?"

"Trailing behind. As usual. They're going to get wet if they don't hurry. A cold drizzle has started." She followed Kate to the kitchen. "Now aren't you glad I insisted you buy that yellow outfit? It's much prettier than the drab brown one you wanted to get. I don't know where you got your sense of style. It wasn't from me."

Kate held her tongue, refusing to let her mother pick a fight with her on Christmas Day. She set the casserole on the kitchen counter as her father and brother brought in two large cloth-covered baskets.

Billy shot her a quizzical look. "What did you do to yourself, Kate? You look sorta decent for a change."

"Merry Christmas to you, too, Billy." She turned to her father. "Hi, Daddy."

He gave her a quick hug, then pushed his glasses up on his nose and studied her. "There *is* something different about you."

Kate touched her hair.

"You cut it, didn't you? I bet your neck gets cold after being used to it long." He turned to his sister-in-law. "Merry Christmas, Ellendor. Rob in his office? I brought him a new computer program."

Billy and her father left the kitchen.

Aunt El gave Kate's mother a hug. "How do you like Kate's new hairdo, Joyce?"

Her mother turned from the basket she was unpacking. "I must say it's an improvement." She scrutinized Kate. "She looks a lot like Sonja with her hair short."

Kate picked up a stack of salad bowls from the counter and took them to the dining room. *You look sorta decent. I bet your neck gets cold. It's a big improvement. She looks like her big sister.* Well, she didn't dress in a new outfit, put on makeup and style her hair for them. She did it for herself.

And she wasn't going to let anyone spoil Christmas for her. She had attended an inspiring Christmas program last night at the church. Amy and little Tommy would be here soon to open the gifts she'd bought them—and Steve would be back in two days.

Dinner went smoothly without her dropping one speck of food in her lap, and no one insulted her while they ate. She was helping clear the table when Sonja's little Amy ran into the kitchen and tugged on her sweater. "Auntie Kate, will you read to me and Tommy?"

The children fell asleep before Kate was through reading the story. Closing the book, she placed it on the bedside table and headed down the hall to help Aunt El finish up in the kitchen.

Passing her uncle Rob's office, she heard her mother's voice inside. "I still can't understand why Father did what he did. I just hope Kate never finds out."

Kate stopped. *Hope Kate never finds out?*

She stepped closer to the opening in the doorway. Her mother and uncles stood beside the desk studying a large sheet of paper.

"It can be easily remedied. There's this little stretch right here." Uncle Rob pointed to a spot on the paper. "We can deed this to Kate. Sonja can do the paperwork. The lot adjoins Charlotte's property on one side and Billy's on the other. Renae's is here and…" His voice faded.

"Kate! Is that you?" Her mother's head appeared around the door. "Are you out there eavesdropping? This is a private conversation."

Kate pushed the door open wider. Her mother stepped back to keep it from hitting her.

"Private, Mother?" Kate kept her voice calm and cool. "What is it you don't want Kate to know?" She looked at her uncles. "Uncle Rob? Uncle Sid?"

The men looked at each other, then at their sister. "Joyce…?"

"Never mind, Robert. I'll handle this." She took Kate's arm and steered her back into the hallway. She closed the door behind them. "I don't know what you think you heard. But you must have misinterpreted it. There's nothing for you to get all worked up about."

"I'm not worked up, Mother. I simply want to know—"

"You'll know when the time comes. Now please go on about your business and let us attend to ours."

Kate took a deep breath and let it out slowly. She would

not let her mother blow her cool. "Yes, Mother, I'll attend to mine."

Back in her bedroom, she gathered her jacket, shoulder bag and umbrella, then slipped out the back door and ran to her car through a sheet of cold rain.

She opened her cell phone and called up a number. "Mr. Boyer, there's something suspicious going on concerning Grandpa's property. I need to know what it is."

He cleared his throat. "Yes, I, uh… Where are you now? Can you drive out to my place?"

When she hesitated, he added, "I have something to show you. You can pull up to the side entrance where my home office is located."

"It's Christmas Day. How about your family?"

"I'm the only one here. We'll have privacy to talk."

Privacy? At his house? After his attitude during their intimate little dinner? She wasn't up for dealing with another complicated relationship. But she needed some answers before her mother and uncles did more damage. Maybe she had just read Mr. Boyer wrong on Tuesday night, and he had not meant anything improper, after all.

"Katerina, are you still there?"

"I'll be there in about fifteen minutes."

She parked the car at the side entrance of the Boyer mansion and grabbed her umbrella. Paul Boyer opened the door as she ran up the steps. "Come on in."

A fire crackled in a large marble fireplace in the room behind him. Classical music played on a stereophonic sound system. Kate shook rain off the umbrella and stepped inside. She looked down at the soft beige carpet under her feet.

"Don't mind the rug. Here, let me take your coat."

He placed her umbrella in a stand beside the door and helped her out of her jacket, which he hung on a brass hanger above the umbrella stand. "Now go warm yourself by the fire."

She glanced round the room as she moved shivering toward the fireplace.

A large, dark wood desk and a table holding a computer, printer and scanner sat beside a wall lined with glass-fronted bookcases. An entertainment center, bar and wine rack occupied the opposite wall. A plush beige sofa and small table sat on one side of the fireplace. Two matching chairs with a table between them occupied the other side.

Paul Boyer smiled at her and moved toward the bar. He wore tan chinos and shirt topped by a sea-green pullover sweater. It was the first time Kate had seen him when he wasn't wearing a crisp white dress shirt and tie.

"How about something to warm you up?" He pulled a bottle from the rack.

Kate shook her head. "No, thank you."

"Something warm?"

"No. I want to see what you have to show me." She turned her back to the fire.

He nodded, replaced the bottle and retrieved a half-empty wineglass from the bar. He picked up an envelope from the desk and moved to the sofa.

Seating himself on the sofa, he set his glass aside and patted a spot beside him. "Have a seat."

Kate sat on the edge of the plush sofa and waited as he pulled a legal-size sheet of paper from the envelope.

He unfolded it. "This is a copy of your grandfather's will."

Grandpa's will! How long had he had this?

Kate took the paper from his hand and read in stunned silence:

I hereby bequeath all my earthly possessions, real and other property, to my three children, Joycelyn

Priscilla Sanderson, Robert L. Cummins and Sidney
Leon Cummins, with the stipulation that they deed…

Kate took a deep breath. *Now he'll mention me.* She
picked up reading.

…with the stipulation that they deed plots of land,
each equal to one-half acre, for the purpose of building homes, to my grandchildren…

Kate read the names, then reread and counted them.
She scanned the remainder of the document before looking at the attorney. "Grandpa had seven grandchildren. He
only listed six."

She counted the names on her fingers as she read them
aloud: "Julia Ann Madison, Thomas Cummins and Renae
Cummins—that's Uncle Sid's three. Charlotte Lucas, Uncle
Rob's daughter. My sister, Sonja Ellis, and my brother, Billy
Sanderson. Six of them. My name's not there. He left me
out."

Too shocked to cry, she stared at Paul. "I don't understand."

"I'm sorry." Paul laid his hand on hers where it rested
between them on the sofa. "I thought maybe you would give
up trying to take the place without ever having to know."

"I don't understand it. I thought Grandpa wanted me to
have his home."

She looked at the document again. It was dated the day
before her grandfather's first stroke. His two old army buddies who'd visited him that week had witnessed it. The re-
cording date was three days *after* the stroke.

This was probably why he'd wanted her to drive him
down to the county seat. Then he'd had the stroke and
ended up in the hospital. She would have been driving him

to the courthouse to record a will leaving land to every grandchild except her.

How could Grandpa do such a thing? How could he forget all about me when I'm the only one who took care of him?

Paul was watching her, compassion in his expression. She swallowed hard, trying to steel herself against the disappointment and pain. "Mother must have found the will when she came and got his checkbook the day of the stroke, then took it and had it recorded."

"She had power of attorney," Paul said gently.

Kate dropped her head to hide her tears. One lone tear dropped onto the document.

Paul took it from her and laid it on the table, then pulled her into his arms. "I'm sorry I had to hurt you. I wish there was some way I could make it better."

She dropped her forehead to his shoulder. He wasn't her boss tonight; he wasn't her lawyer. He was a kind and gentle man. And he was here.

Gentle fingers lifted her chin and turned her face up to his. His lips moved toward hers.

"No, Paul." She turned her face from his and pushed against his chest with her hands. "Let me go."

He took his arms away and she jumped to her feet.

When he reached for his wineglass, she moved toward the door.

She paused beside the coatrack and pulled a tissue from her pocket.

His hands dropped onto her shoulders. "You're in no shape to drive, and it's still storming. You should stay until it lightens up."

"I'll be all right." She lifted her jacket from the rack.

He took it from her hands. "Don't go yet."

She wiped her nose on the tissue. "I can't stay." She reached for the coat.

He held it for her to slip into it and then placed his hands on her shoulders again. When his lips touched the back of her neck, she shrugged his hands away.

She pulled her umbrella from the stand and reached for the doorknob.

Opening the door as jagged lightning flashed across the sky and a clap of thunder shook the windows, he quickly closed the door. "You can't leave in this."

"I have to go."

"Then let me take you. I'll get—"

"No. I drove myself out here, I'll drive myself home. Let me leave."

He opened the door and she dashed for her car with the umbrella unopened. She slid inside her car.

Too many confusing, distressing things had happened here today. She had to get away from him. From the things he told her. The things he did.

Everything was confusing. It was still too early to be so dark, yet darkness, broken only by streaks of lightning, blanketed everything. *Like the day Jesus died.*

She moved at a snail's pace through a new and strange world as she made her way down the circular driveway to the main road. Grandpa had forgotten her. Or deliberately left her out. Why would he do such a thing? Did she mean so little to him? Had he never loved her as she thought he did?

Kate wasn't sure where she was headed through the blinding rain. But it didn't matter. Nothing mattered anymore. Her world with all her dreams had just come crashing down around her.

Chapter 17

Kate climbed out of the car and peered into the darkness. Rain poured over her head and down the collar of her jacket. Thunder crashed about her. Lightning illuminated white stones on the hillside.

If she could only talk to her grandfather, he would explain everything. If she could get up the muddy hillside and find his grave in the darkness.

She picked up a foot and set it down—into a puddle of water. She picked it up and set it down again, her shoe mired in mud. She pulled her shoe out of the mud, stepped again and slipped, hitting the ground on all fours.

It was no use. She couldn't do it. Like everything else in her life, this was impossible, too.

She struggled to her feet and clomped back to her car, her shoes heavy with mud.

She turned the key in the ignition, but the car refused to start. She tried again and the motor caught.

Back at her aunt's house, she couldn't get the key into

the lock on the door. After several tries she realized she was trying to insert the car key.

After finally getting the door open, she picked up a foot to step inside and discovered globs of mud clinging to her shoes. Kicking the shoes off, she left them on the porch.

"Kate, is that you? Are you all right? Your mother wants you to call her on her cell. She got worried about you after you left in the storm."

The voice came from someplace in the distance. Kate tried to focus on the words and form an answer. "I'm all right, Aunt El. Will you call her? I need a hot bath."

She stood under the shower, letting it beat down upon her until the water ran cold, but she still couldn't get warm. She slipped beneath the covers, shivering.

When she closed her eyes, words from her grandfather's Last Will and Testament appeared on the inside of her eyelids. *To my grandchildren…*

All the names were there except mine.

I know the plans I have for you, says the Lord, plans to give you a future and a hope.

Why did the Scripture keep haunting her? Why wouldn't it go away? Her plans were now hopeless, her hope for the future gone. And all the time she'd spent with Grandpa left a bitter taste in her mouth.

He had given away the house where he'd raised his family, where Kate had spent so many happy hours. The woods she loved to tramp through. The stream where she learned to swim. The old tree where she sat to write and draw…

And now it had all been sold by people who didn't want or appreciate it.

Of course, she wouldn't have met Steve if they hadn't sold the land to him. Still, it hurt.

It hurts so much that he just forgot about me.

Barely able to croak next morning, she staggered into

the kitchen where her aunt sat at the table with a cup of coffee and the morning paper.

"Kate," her aunt exclaimed. "You look like death warmed over. Get back in bed. I'll bring a thermometer."

"Sore throat," Kate croaked, clasping a hand around her neck before stumbling back to the bedroom.

The medicine Aunt El gave her put her to sleep for most of the day and all night.

She woke on Sunday morning to a bright, sunny sky. Her temperature was down, her throat much better and she could talk without sounding like a frog.

Her boss called as she was about to leave for Steve's house. "How about dinner, Katerina?"

"Thank you, but I have plans."

"Can't you change them? We may need to discuss the will."

"Thanks, but I know all I need to know about the will, and I can't change my plans. I'll see you tomorrow at the office."

Steve's double-cab pickup was parked beside the house. When she didn't find him in the house or yard, she set out for his old campsite. She would tell him she knew the place was legally his. And if he cared about her the way his actions sometimes implied, there was now nothing to stand between them.

She set out in a run between the trees.

But just as she was about to step into the clearing, a voice stopped her.

"Did you find him?"

It was Steve's voice. Someone was with him at the campsite.

A child giggled. "He was playing with a lizard."

"He was *not* playing with it," another childish voice said. "He was *pointing* at it."

Kate moved cautiously behind a bush and peered through.

A boy about four or five years old struggled to hold on to a spotted puppy.

A girl, probably a little older, stood with hands propped on plump, little hips. "He was not pointing at it. Dogs can't point."

"Silly. Pointing don't mean he's—pointing. He don't have fingers. He's pointing his *nose* at it."

Feminine laughter mingled with Steve's.

Kate's head jerked round.

Steve and a dark-haired young woman stood on the far side of the clearing, his arm draped across her shoulders.

Kate's mouth dropped open as the little girl ran to them. "Mommy, Freddy called me silly."

"You shouldn't call your sister names, Freddy. And please put the puppy down before he tears your jacket with his squirming."

The boy put the dog on the ground, pointed a finger at him and commanded, "Stay, Nickel!"

The puppy sat wagging his tail, watching his young master explain in detail how a dog "points" at something with its nose instead of a finger.

Instead of listening, the little girl skipped off to chase falling leaves.

The woman grinned at Steve. "Just like you. Always ready with a detailed explanation."

Steve laughed. "I was thinking how much he reminds me of Dad."

"Like father, like son."

He laughed again and turned her toward the hillock where Kate had chopped up the stakes he'd used to lay out a building. "Come let me show you where the house will be."

Kate came out of her daze. So that's who he was planning to build a house for! She was glad she'd chopped up his stakes. She wished there were more she could attack.

She would like to attack him. Why had he led her on the way he had when he was obviously a married man? Why had he kissed her? Why had he made her fall in love with him?

So, there was nothing to stand between them now, was there? Sure. Nothing but a wife and two kids. How could she have been so foolish as to let herself fall in love with a married man?

She turned and crashed through the bushes, back toward her car. In her aunt and uncle's driveway, she sat pounding the steering wheel, fighting tears. Then, lifting her head and squaring her shoulders, she mumbled aloud, "Well, I don't need you, Steve Adams. I have other options."

She pulled her cell phone from her bag and punched in a number.

"Paul? If that invitation for dinner is still open, I'll take you up on it."

"Sounds good. Just one problem. The kids came home early. How about pizza here?"

His house with the kids?

"I could cook something, if Lisa wants to help me." Cooking and Lisa's chatter would help occupy her mind and fill up the evening.

"Sounds good. Lisa, do you want to help Miss Sanderson cook?"

"Kate? Sure. I'll help her. Can I talk to her?" Lisa's voice came over the line. "Hi, Kate. Can we have fried chicken?"

"Sure. I'll stop by the grocery store on my way."

Later, while Lisa rolled chicken parts in a mixture of flour, salt and pepper, Kate heated oil in a skillet on the range top. She didn't often eat fried foods anymore, but after all she'd been through lately, she deserved to coddle herself a bit.

"Mrs. Mason uses the deep fryer to make fried chicken." Flour decorated Lisa's cheeks, hair and the work island.

Kate smiled at her. "This is the old-fashioned way."

A pensive look replaced Lisa's smile. "I wish Mommy made fried chicken. She doesn't like to cook. Did your mom teach you?"

"No. My grandfather. Do you have the chicken ready to put in the pan? The oil is hot."

"Coming right up." Lisa bounced to the stove with the bowl of floured chicken.

A short while later, Kate, Paul and his kids sat at his kitchen table, their hunger sated.

Paul Jr. turned a picked-clean chicken drumstick in his hands, checking to be sure he had not missed a morsel. "Mrs. Mason's fried chicken don't have bones to lick."

"That's because she doesn't use the real thing," Lisa said. "And doesn't cook it the old way like Kate does. Isn't this a great dinner, Daddy? I helped with the chicken, the potatoes and the salad. But Kate made the gravy. And the biscuits. She makes them the old way, too."

Paul smiled across the table at Kate. "The best I've had in a long time."

"I wish Mom could cook chicken like this," his son said. "Don't you, Dad?"

He glanced at his father and laid the chicken leg on his plate. "I just wish she'd come home and cook something. Even her burned smashed taters." His face brightened. "Maybe Kate could come regular and cook for us. Wouldn't that be great, Dad? I bet you'd stay home more if Kate was here."

"I bet I would, too, son." He shot Kate an intense look.

She pushed back her chair. "If all of you are finished, I'll clear the table. Maybe you have a table game we can play after we fill the dishwasher." She looked from one child to the other.

"I do, I do." Paul Jr. jumped to his feet, the bare drumstick in his hand. He gave it one more nibble and laid it on his plate. "I'll get it."

"I have a really good one," Lisa said. "Let's play mine first. I helped cook dinner."

Their dad cleared his throat. "I thought you two might want to watch a movie while Katerina and I talk in my office."

Kate grinned at him. "What's the matter? You afraid we'll beat you?"

Lisa gave him a coy look. "Yeah, Daddy, are you afraid we'll beat you? I've never seen you play a game."

"I can play games."

"Come on, Dad," his son coaxed. "Let's show these girls we can beat 'em."

Paul laughed and picked up his plate. "Okay. Let's help Kate clear the table first."

Kate managed to *almost* put Steve out of her mind while she laughed and played with Paul and his kids.

About ten o'clock Paul pushed back his chair. "It's bedtime, kids. Put the game up and tell Katerina good-night."

Paul Jr. gave his father a pleading look. "Aw, Dad, just as we were getting good."

"Just one more game?" Lisa begged. "We don't have school tomorrow."

"But Katerina and I have work."

"Ooo-kay." They spoke in unison as they began gathering up game pieces. Each gave Kate a quick hug and dragged toward the stairs.

Before the kids disappeared around the upstairs landing, Paul Jr. called back, "Hey, Dad, I bet we'll beat 'em next time."

Grinning, Paul slipped an arm around Kate's shoulders. "Let's sit by the fire and relax with something to drink."

She took his hand away. "I'd better get home."

As she lifted her jacket from the rack by his office door, he took it from her, then leaned over and kissed her neck.

She stiffened. He spoke close to her ear. "The kids love you, Katerina. You look right standing at my stove."

She gave a shaky laugh. "Are you suggesting I become your cook instead of your legal assistant?"

"You know what I mean."

She faced him. "I'm much too tired, physically and emotionally, to deal with anything more tonight, Paul."

"I want to help you deal with it, Katerina."

"You're grateful to me for helping with your kids. And for helping out in your office. That's all."

She reached for her jacket, and he held it for her to slip into. She pulled a scarf from a pocket and tied it around her hair.

"You're covering that beautiful head."

"My ears get cold. I think I'll grow my hair out again. I'm beginning to miss it."

He touched her cheek. "I like the new Katerina."

"I'm not new. I'm the same person. I just look different." She turned toward the door.

"I can see about contesting the will."

"No. If this is what Grandpa wanted…"

"People often have ministrokes before having major ones. Your grandfather's mind may have been impaired by one when he made the will. Are you familiar with the people who witnessed it? You said they were your grandfather's old army buddies."

"Mr. Bennett lived in Birmingham. The other one lived somewhere out of state."

"I should be able to locate Bennett and see what he has to say." He touched her arm. "For now, put it out of your mind while I work on it. How about a New Year's Eve party

Thursday night? A lawyer friend invited me, said bring someone."

New Year's Eve? I wonder what Steve... She shook her head. "Thanks. But I...already have an invitation for a New Year's Eve party."

She didn't tell him it was at the church and she didn't plan to go. And she no longer had hopes of Steve asking her out.

Chapter 18

Steve threw another log on the fire and sat down in the rocking chair. Here it was New Year's Eve and he sat all alone brooding, watching sparks fly up the chimney. He had tried to call Kate several times since he'd come back from Christmas in Georgia with his family. But she never answered the phone or the messages he left.

Was she angry with him or just tired of his company? Maybe she'd learned about the will and given up on taking the land. Or maybe she was out with another man. Her aunt had said she was having dinner with friends when he'd called Sunday evening.

I don't like football and I don't have a boyfriend, she'd told him the day she'd burst in on him at his campsite. But she could have met someone since then.

Stop fretting about it, Steve. You don't have a claim on her just because you have her house.

But suppose she's sick...

He'd try calling one more time, and if he didn't get her this time, he'd go over to the house.

She answered on the first ring.

"Katie! I'm glad I caught you. You haven't returned my calls."

"I've been sort of—tied up."

"Tied up?"

"Yeah. You know, with—things. Not the same kind of things you have. Not with— the same kind of people."

People? Had she learned what he did for a living? "Katie…?"

"I'll be really busy for a while, Steve. Classes start back next week. I guess I won't be dropping in on you anymore when you're—busy."

"I'm never too busy for you, Katie. As a matter of fact, I thought—if you're not busy tonight…"

"I am busy. I had an invitation to a party at an attorney's house."

"I see." A picture of the slick-talking Paul Boyer popped into his head. Was she going out with her boss? He'd heard the man was divorced.

"Do you think we might get together before you return to school?"

"I'm leaving this weekend and I have a lot to do to get ready. So this is goodbye, Steve. I hope things work out well for you and…" He thought he heard a catch in her voice as she broke the connection.

And her goodbye sounded so final.

He'd thought they were becoming friends. Maybe a little more than friends. At least learning to get along. He thought he was getting to know her well. Now he felt he didn't know her at all. What had happened with her while he was away those few days?

He backtracked in his mind to the last time they were together. It was the night they decorated the tree and went to Vulcan. They'd had such a good time together. Or at least, he thought she had, too. She had avoided his good-night kiss when he'd opened the car door for her, but she hadn't appeared angry.

He placed the phone on the table beside the rocking chair and sat frowning into the fire. What did she mean by his being tied up? What—or who—did she think he'd been tied up with? What had she started to say but hadn't finished?

He shook his head and stood. Would he ever figure her out? Would he ever get a chance to try, with her avoiding him?

Looks like I may as well take down the tree. From the sound of things, all the needles would die and fall off before she came again.

Kate taped the last box shut and glanced around the tiny apartment. "And thus closes another sad chapter of my life. I hope the next one is better than the last one."

She picked up the box and trudged down the stairs.

A couple she had seen around the dorm swung through the front door of the building. The girl stepped aside while the guy held the door open for Kate. "Need some help?"

"Thanks. This is the last one."

As the door closed between them, she heard the girl call, "Race you up the stairs."

Kate stood on the little porch, holding the box, listening to their footsteps pound up the inside steps and their laughter float back down. Would she ever have such a carefree and happy relationship?

She couldn't imagine ever being as happy again as she'd been the night she and Steve had stood together under the stars at Vulcan Park. And ate hot dogs while sitting cozily in his pickup atop Red Mountain.

How quickly that bubble had burst.

Sighing, she hefted the box onto her hip, then trudged across the icy ground toward her car.

When she reached her aunt's house, her mother's car was sitting in the driveway. "Is that you, Kate?" Her mother walked out of the kitchen and followed her into the bedroom.

"I brought you this." She handed Kate a folded paper.

Kate sat on the bed and unfolded it. *A deed!*

It was signed by her mother and uncles.

"Thank you, Mother, but I won't need it. I'll not be *playing in the dirt* anymore. I'm not going back to school." She held the document out to her.

Her mother drew back and glared at her. "Not going back! You're telling me you're going to waste all the time and money you spent there the past three and a half years?"

"It won't all be wasted. I can still use the things I learned in business classes. That's what you suggested, isn't it?"

Her mother nodded and sat down beside Kate. "That seems best to me. Find out what else you need to take to get a business degree. You can transfer to the University of Alabama instead of going back to that cow college."

"Mother! It's a good school. It…" She stopped. *Lord, give me patience.*

She tried again. "I appreciate what you're trying to do. And I'm sorry I was so rude to you. But I don't want the land this way." *Especially since Grandpa didn't care enough to leave me part of it.* She dropped the deed onto the bed between them.

"Kate, don't be difficult. It's already done." She picked up the deed and pressed it into Kate's hand. "I insist you take this and then get yourself to the University of Alabama first thing Monday morning and see if you can salvage some of the time you've wasted down there."

Kate watched her mother flounce from the room and slam the door behind her.

"I don't want a business degree, Mother. I'm not transferring to the University of Alabama."

She glanced at the paper in her hand. Maybe she *would* keep the deed and sell the little plot of land like her mother had sold the rest.

Then, after Jane had her baby and got back to work, Kate could use the money to go off someplace and work with her art for a while.

Jane's baby was born at the end of January. Kate agreed to work every day until Jane's doctor allowed her to return to the office.

Driving past Steve's driveway on those cold winter evenings, her eyes searched out his lights through bare tree limbs in the gray evening stillness. Oftentimes, she detected a swirl of dark smoke above the trees. But she resisted the urge to drive down the hill and join him at his fireside.

Occasionally, she accepted Paul's offer to dinner at a nice restaurant. Quite often she picked up food at the grocery store on the way to his house, where she and Lisa cooked a meal together. Sometimes she, Paul and the kids played a game after dinner. At other times, she helped Pauley or Lisa with homework while their father worked on legal documents in his study. But as soon as Paul sent the kids off to bed, she insisted she had to leave.

He didn't try to talk her into staying longer and made no more inappropriate suggestions. At the office, he behaved professionally.

But each time she left his house, or he left her at her front door, he took her arm, leaned over and planted a quick kiss on her cheek. Kate allowed this and came to expect it. But she didn't invite more.

Then, on Thursday morning, before Jane was due back in the office the following Monday, he walked into the outer office while Kate was proofing a report she had printed.

"A Midsummer Night's Dream is playing at the Alabama Shakespeare Festival this week. Do you think you might like to go see it tonight?"

"Tonight?" Kate's hand went instinctively to her hair. "In Montgomery?"

"We can close the office this afternoon. Your hair looks fine."

Kate studied his face as he waited for her answer. She had seen the lighthearted comedy as a college sophomore and would love to see it again. But could she trust Paul to keep his distance with her? Did he have another motive for asking her? She decided to take the risk. After all, he wasn't leading her on like some people. She shook her head to clear the thought. When would she get over Steve?

Chapter 19

Green silk swished about Kate's nylon-clad legs as she walked briskly from the ladies' room and across the theater lobby. She paused to glance around her. By which door had Paul said to meet him?

Stopping abruptly, she turned to look behind her—and bumped into a broad masculine chest clad in a white shirt and dark coat.

"Oh, I'm sorry. I…" She looked up and gasped. There, staring down at her, was a pair of startling blue eyes above a neatly trimmed beard. "Steve?"

The eyes widened. "Katie?" The man clasped her arm. "It is you. Your hair…"

Steve, in a tuxedo. Looking so handsome she thought her heart would melt. Or pound right out of her chest. She willed her legs to regain their strength.

She attempted a cool smile. "Oh, yes, I forgot you haven't seen my haircut." She tilted her chin and touched her hair, which now curled around her cheeks and neck. "It has grown out some."

"Grown out? It was shorter? You cut it *all* off?"

"Oh, yes. It was quite short." Proud she was able to appear so calm on the outside while being so flustered on the inside, she offered him another smile and attempted to pull her arm from his grasp. "It's good to see you, Steve, but someone is waiting for me."

"Oh? Who?" He glanced round them. "Where…?"

"I have to go."

"Wait." He released her arm and grabbed her hand. "Come meet someone."

She held back. "No. I…"

"It will only take a minute." He pulled her with him, threading a way for them through people milling about the lobby.

He led her to the spot where two women and a man stood together. "Folks, this is Katie."

"Kate, it's so good to finally meet you." The woman from the woods hugged her, a broad smile lighting her face.

Baffled, Kate looked from the woman to Steve.

Steve opened his mouth to speak, but the woman laughed and spoke first. "I've heard so much about you I feel like I know you. I'm Elizabeth."

Elizabeth. So his wife's name was Elizabeth?

Steve was grinning from ear to ear. "Didn't I tell you she was something? But the hair…"

Kate caught her bottom lip between her teeth. She reached up and touched her hair. Had her wild mane been some kind of joke with him?

Elizabeth touched her arm. "Don't let his teasing bother you, Kate."

Chuckling, he turned to the man and woman standing beside Elizabeth. "Katie, this is Melissa Willis and Fred."

The two smiled and extended hands for Kate to take.

Flustered, Kate shook hands with the couple. Was Steve Adams a born flirt and she had never before realized it? Or had he just been trying to soften her up with all his attentions in order to divert her attention from attempts to take back her family's land? Either way, it was evident he had been talking to his wife about her. She wondered if he'd told Elizabeth he'd kissed her.

"Don't you think so, Kate?"

At the sound of her name, Kate blinked her eyes and shook her head, trying to clear the confusion in her brain. "Oh, uh, I'm sorry. I guess I…"

"There you are, Katerina. I thought I had lost you."

Kate glanced round as a hand touched her shoulder. "Paul!" She glanced at the others.

Steve's eyes narrowed. The smile left his face.

"Th-this is my bo…" She stopped and steadied her voice. "This is Paul Boyer. Mr. Boyer, this is Stephen Adams and his… Elizabeth. And Fred and…Melissa?"

Melissa nodded.

Paul reached out to shake hands with Steve. "Adams, I…"

"Excuse me." Kate laid a hand on Paul's arm. "I think it's time to go back to our seats." She brushed between Paul and Steve and headed across the lobby.

"Katerina." Paul caught her arm. "Slow down. You're going the wrong way."

Steve watched Kate move away from him with Paul Boyer holding her arm. So, she was going out with him. That's what had been keeping her busy. And he'd thought she was away at school.

"Is that someone special?" Melissa asked. "Or should I ask?"

"Only the love of Steve's life," Fred said.

Steve was still watching Kate's bright head disappear among the crowd.

"Don't tease him, Fred." Elizabeth took Steve's arm. "Come on, Stevie. Let's go finish watching the play."

Kate settled into her seat and took a deep breath as the curtain went up. So far, the performance had been light-hearted and fun. Now the drama onstage seemed dull compared to the real-life drama out in the lobby.

She wondered where they were sitting, and glanced around the theater. But it was too dark to see much.

Turning back toward the stage, she found Paul looking at her.

"They're across the aisle, two rows up," he whispered, leaning his head close to hers.

Kate felt herself blush. "Who? I wasn't…"

"Shh." He took her hand.

Kate let him hold it but couldn't resist glancing at the section of seats he'd indicated.

Her eyes met Steve's across a row of heads, and her face grew hot.

Was he searching her out, too?

Their eyes locked for a moment, tension radiating across the room between them. Then Steve smiled and, although she couldn't tell for sure in the dimness, she thought he winked.

And she flushed again, this time with anger. How dare he try to flirt with her when he was with another woman—his wife, no less.

With a toss of her head, she turned her eyes back toward the stage. Shifting her shoulders, she leaned lightly into Paul.

Paul clasped her hand a little tighter and looked at her. "You okay?"

She gave him a bright smile. "I'm great."

But she could not concentrate on the play—until words of Shakespeare's lovesick Helena caught her attention. "You draw me, you hard-hearted adamant…"

Kate's heart echoed the words: *You draw me, you hard-hearted adamant,* and she stifled an urge to cry along with poor Helena, who now pleaded with her "heart's desire" to give up the power he had over her.

"Do I entice you…?" the hard-hearted Demetrius shouted at the weeping girl onstage.

Yes, Kate's traitorous heart whispered. *You do entice me, Stephen Adams, with the way you smile, the way you speak, the way you look at me....*

"…Do I not in plainest truth tell you, I do not, nor I cannot love you?"

No, Steve. You never said you cannot love me. You never told me you love someone else. That you have a wife.

Instead, Steve had kissed her, cooked for her and taken care of her as no one ever had before. He had touched her and tended her injuries more tenderly than anyone else ever had. He had treated her as though she were someone special to him.

And she had come to believe it might be true. Then, she'd learned he was married and had tried to do the honorable thing by staying away from him. But would he let her? No. He'd harassed her on the telephone by continuing to call her. And now he had the nerve to smile and wink at her in a crowded room.

She glanced across the darkened theater to where he sat now, just as he leaned over to whisper something in the ear of the dark-haired woman sitting beside him.

Kate took a quivering breath and bit her bottom lip to prevent it from escaping audibly. *You have only been playing with my silly schoolgirl heart, Stephen Adams. But no more. Don't you dare ever speak to me again.*

She pulled her hand from Paul's and stifled a sob as she searched frantically in her tiny black bag for a tissue.

When a masculine hand pressed a crisp white handkerchief into her hand, she took it numbly and lifted it to her dripping nose. "Thank you," she mumbled on a quivery breath, without looking at the man beside her. She blotted tears from her cheeks and wiped her nose again.

When she finally squelched her tears enough to look up, Paul was studying her. His lips twisted in a slight smile.

Kate sniffled again and tried to smile as she reached the handkerchief out to him.

He patted her hand. "Keep it."

She nodded and touched the square of linen to her eyes.

The elderly woman on the other side of her patted her hand. "It's all right, dear," she whispered. "I cry when I read Shakespeare."

Kate hoped Paul thought her tears were for poor Helena, too, instead of realizing she was crying over another man.

Well, they were the last tears she'd ever shed over that cheating louse, she promised herself.

She sat up straighter in her seat and turned her attention back to the stage, where the lovesick Helena and hardhearted Demetrius had exited the woods and the stage. Fairies were now devising a way to make Demetrius fall in love with Helena.

Kate wiped her eyes again. If only a flower could so easily make Steve love her. But even a real miracle couldn't erase the fact that he was married.

After the final curtain call, Paul's hand on her elbow guided her out to the aisle away from Steve and his group, then through the crowd and out to his car.

Settling into the deep upholstery of the Lexus, she leaned her head back and closed her eyes. The strain of this night had exhausted her.

She jolted alert when the car stopped. They sat in a hotel

parking lot. "How about a bite to eat? The hotel has a great restaurant." He slipped a hand to the back of her neck and began slowly massaging it. "You've seemed a little tense since intermission."

She leaned back against his hand and closed her eyes. The muscles in her neck were beginning to relax.

"They also have Jacuzzis…."

The hot water would feel great…. "I think we'd better go. It's getting late."

"And soft beds…"

Her eyes flew open. She jerked his hand from her neck. "Start the car, please, Paul! And take me home."

He caught her fingers with his and held them. "How long have we been seeing each other, Katerina?"

"Well, let's see," she said icily. "I first came to your office the day after Thanksgiving…."

"That's not what I mean, and you know it." He released her fingers. "Do you ever think about where this… relationship is heading?"

"Heading? What do you mean? Why does it have to head someplace? Why can't we just be employer and employee—and friends who enjoy each other's company? And your kids when they are with us?"

She added the last as a reminder that he wasn't some young playboy but a father responsible for the welfare of two children. "Don't you need to check on Lisa and Paul Jr.?"

He smoothed the fabric of her coat sleeve. "Mrs. Mason is with them. Is this the coat you bought when you and Lisa went shopping together? With my credit card?"

She yanked her arm away from his hand. If she didn't think she'd freeze before she got home, she would rip the coat off and give it back to him. "Start the car, Paul. It's cold in here."

He gave her a wry smile in the light from the parking lot. "I noticed."

Close to tears, Kate leaned back in the car seat, hugging herself with arms clothed in the coat he'd bought. A *bonus* for her work in his office, he'd said. Now he expected her to pay for it with a night in a five-star hotel and a Jacuzzi? This whole time he hadn't been pushing her for more intimacy, he'd been biding his time, waiting for such an opportunity as this.

"You're in love with Adams, aren't you?"

She bit her lip before she answered. "Yes." *Not that it will do me any good.* "I'm sorry, Paul." *But I wouldn't be spending the night with you, even if I wasn't.*

He started the car. "I'm sorry, too."

When they were out on the open road he put a CD in the player.

"My heart cries for you..."

He pushed a button and changed the disc. They pretended to listen to jazz piano and big band all the way home.

When Paul stopped in her aunt's driveway, Kate opened the car door. "Good night, Mr. Boyer. Thank you for an interesting—and enlightening—evening. You don't have to walk me to the door."

He nodded and she got out of the car.

She didn't go into the office the next morning until it was time for him to be at a meeting. She would gather her personal belongings from her desk drawer and leave him a note—and let him make do the best he could until Jane came back to the office.

When the phone rang, she let the machine take it. "I need to leave a message for Kate Sanderson, please."

Kate grabbed the receiver. "Steve! Why are you calling me at the office? What do you want?" How could her voice sound so steady when her bones were jelly?

"You wouldn't return my earlier calls to your home, so I thought I'd try to catch you at work. There are some people I want you to meet."

"I did that last night, remember? At the theater."

He laughed. "This is someone else." He sounded a little shaky, too.

He was nervous about introducing her to his kids. He probably thought if she met them, she wouldn't have the heart to take away the land and deprive them of the house he wanted to build for them and their mother. He didn't know she was no longer looking for a way to take the place or that she had seen her grandfather's will.

"They're coming over from Atlanta in the morning. Will you come?"

"I don't think so. I—have things to do." It had been difficult enough meeting Steve's wife. She didn't want to have to smile and make small talk with his kids while her heart broke all over again.

"You won't have to stay long."

Kate took a deep breath and held it for a long moment before she let it out. She may as well go on and get it over with. How much worse could it be than meeting their mother? After all, she had already seen the children.

She took a deep, shaky breath. "All right, Steve." After tomorrow she would finally put Steve behind her and move on. But move on to where?

Chapter 20

Kate heard children's voices as she walked up Steve's steps the next day. They sure were a noisy pair. Or else he had more kids than she realized.

The door flew open. "Katie! Come in."

It was Elizabeth. Now *she* was using Grandpa's pet name for her.

Kate stepped inside, and the room went quiet. Several young boys, and the little girl Kate had seen in the woods, stared at her.

Oh, my, he has a houseful of kids.

The children sat on benches with a board game spread out on the table in front of them. The table looked like the one Steve had used in the woods. Only now, it and the benches sported a shiny coat of white paint.

A plump, older woman with a kind, motherly smile rocked a curly-haired toddler beside a dying fire in the fireplace. The delicious aroma of vegetable soup filled the room.

Elizabeth met her at the door smiling. "Let me take your coat." Feeling suddenly too warm, Kate gladly shed her jacket.

Elizabeth reached for it. "I'll hang it on a chair for you. I'm afraid the rack is full." She nodded at the small jackets and caps hanging on the clothes tree by the door. "Steve and Dad walked out to the building site. Steve said if you came before he gets back to tell you he'll only be a few minutes. He had to show a deliveryman where to unload building materials."

Building site. Building materials. Kate felt the color drain from her face.

Elizabeth didn't seem to notice as she walked toward the fireplace. "Come meet Mom."

Kate followed her on shaky legs. Elizabeth took her arm. Her smile seemed genuine. "Mom, this is Steve's Katie."

Steve's Katie? Couldn't the woman be at least aSTET little bit jealous of her?

The older lady smiled. "I would have known even if you hadn't already called her that, with that beautiful red hair. She's just like Steve described her. Except for the short hair. *Glorious stuff,* Stephen called it. Why did you cut it off, dear?"

Kate blinked and tried to smile. Why was Steve's family making such a fuss about her hair?

"Come over here, Kate, and give me a hug. I can't get up with this sleeping child in my lap. And I don't dare disturb him, poor tyke, after the trouble he has sleeping."

Dazed at their greeting, Kate bent and hugged the lady.

"Now, come meet the kids." Elizabeth took her hand. She introduced the boys as Bobby, Brian, William, George and "my Freddy." She touched the little girl on the head. "And this is Jody. Say hello to Kate, kids."

The older boys, who appeared to be around eight to ten years of age, spoke solemnly in unison, "Hello, Kate."

Freddy looked up from dominoes he was stacking. "Hi, I'm building a fort. See this line right here? It's the wall. You have to have a wall around a fort to keep the enemy out. That's why…"

Just like you, Elizabeth had said to Steve. *Always ready with a detailed explanation.*

"Mommy, Freddy's talking too much again."

Elizabeth laughed. "Be patient, Jody. You'll get your turn. Go ahead, Freddy, finish telling Kate about your fort so your sister can talk."

"The enemy's why I built the wall." He looked at his sister. "And that's all. I don't have it finished yet."

Kate forced a smile. "It's a nice fort. Thank you, Freddy, for telling me about it."

"You're welcome." He went back to his work, and Kate turned to Jody.

"I'm the scorekeeper," the child said. "See." She turned the pad in front of her, where Kate could see what she had written. "I know how to write my numbers and add."

Kate nodded. "You write them very well, Jody. I'm sure your mommy—and daddy are proud of you."

"Daddy says I'm smart." Jody turned her pad around and studied it.

Daddy. Would she ever get used to thinking of Steve as *Daddy?*

The boy called Bobby studied Kate. "Uncle Steve said you're fun."

Uncle Steve. At least this one wasn't Steve's child.

"Smart, too," William added. "You wanna be my partner? I keep losing with George."

George squirmed on the bench. "Yeah, I'm not very good at games." He rubbed one eye with the palm of a hand. "I didn't wanna play anyhow." He stood and laid his game piece on the table.

Poor little fellow. Kate wanted to hug him. He probably

felt as inadequate with the other guys as she had felt with her cousins when she was growing up. "I'll bet George could play with a little help."

She glanced at Elizabeth's mother. What would they think if she sat down and played with the kids instead of visiting with them? Not that it mattered to her what Steve's wife thought.

Both women smiled and nodded at her.

Kate glanced round the table. "I've never played this game. How about if George and I play together while I'm learning?" She winked at George and leaned toward him as if forming a conspiracy. "Maybe together we can beat them."

He grinned, sat down and slid over to make room for Kate.

"Ah, we'll still lose," William complained. "But, okay. You'll probably catch on a lot quicker than George."

"Yeah, I don't read very good," George mumbled as Kate sat down.

"You don't read very *well*," Brian, the one with glasses, corrected. "His English is not too good, either."

"You boys stop picking on George," Elizabeth's mother said. "He's made a lot of progress."

Bobby nodded. "Yeah, he has. When we first come to live with Mama and Papa Ad he wouldn't talk none at all."

Kate glanced from George to Bobby, noting the similarity in their coloring. "Are you two brothers?"

Bobby nodded while George rubbed his right ear with the palm of his hand, his big brown eyes downcast.

"Does your ear bother you?" Kate spoke softly, close to his ear.

He shook his head.

"It's just a habit," Bobby said. "He'll get over it."

"Sure he will." Kate picked up the game piece and handed it to George. "You do the moving, George, and I'll draw a card. We can read together to see what it says we're supposed to do."

They were finishing the first game when the front door opened. "Well, I see you've gotten acquainted with the kids, Katie."

Steve followed a gray-haired gentleman into the room. They shed workmen's gloves and dropped them in the corner under the coatrack.

"Katie, this is my dad." Steve put his hand on the older man's shoulder. "Dad, this is Katie. Kate Sanderson."

Mr. Adams was tall like his son, with a head full of snowy-white hair. Long creases appeared down each bronzed cheek when he smiled. He was dressed like Steve, in denim jeans, heavy boots and bright plaid shirt under a denim jacket.

Looks more like a lumberjack than a preacher. Kate slid off the bench and stood as he extended a hand to her.

"I hear lots of good things about you, Kate Sanderson. It's nice to meet you."

Kate smiled and placed her hand in his. She liked the feel of his strong, sure grip.

Glancing from the man to the woman holding the little boy, she did a quick mental calculation. If this was Steve's dad, then the woman must be his mother. That would make Elizabeth their daughter-in-law instead of their daughter. Well, she knew other people who called their in-laws Mom and Dad. People especially close to their spouse's parents. The thought made her even more jealous of Elizabeth.

"Look, Uncle Steve, Papa Ad." Brian pointed at the score pad. "George is doing better with Kate helping him."

Steve ruffled George's hair. "He's learning more every day, aren't you, buddy?"

George grinned at him.

Steve looked at his mother. "Jamie still having trouble sleeping?"

She nodded.

"Poor child." Papa Ad turned to Kate. "When he first came to us, one of us had to hold him most of the night every night for him to sleep. He's doing a little better now."

A knock sounded on the door, and Elizabeth went to answer it.

"Hello, ma'am. I have a delivery for Dr. Adams. Is he here?" A man stood on the porch with a clipboard in his hand.

Kate glanced at Steve's dad. *Dr. Adams?*

Elizabeth turned to the people in the room. "Steve? There's someone to see you."

At Kate's gasp, Steve looked at her. He shrugged his shoulders, raised his eyebrows and twisted his lips in a wry smile, as if to say, *What can I say?*

Kate gaped at Steve as he signed a form on the man's clipboard.

Steve turned back into the room. "Dad, will you go show him where to take the stuff? Kate, will you come outside with me a minute?"

Kate let Steve lead her out the door. But when the door closed behind them, she jerked her arm from his hand. She planted her hands on her hips and glared at him. "So—*Dr. Stephen Adams*, you work in an office in Birmingham on Tuesdays and Thursdays? Yeah, a *doctor's* office. What kind of doctor are you? Why didn't you want me to know?"

"I'm a psychologist, a therapist, Kate. I counsel people. I use an office at the church where my friend pastors."

"Psychologist! You're a shrink? How long were you planning to use me for your study of neurotic women before you told me what you were up to?"

"See. That's why I didn't tell you. How many times have you put down therapists to me?"

Kate took her hands from her hips and folded her arms. She didn't answer him.

"Kate, there's something else I need to tell you while we're airing things."

"Airing things? That's what you call it? So—tell me."

"Mom, Dad and the boys are coming here to live. We're building them a house. And..."

And you're building one for Elizabeth.

"We're putting up a school building."

"A school?"

"A private Christian school. At first, it'll be for only the homeless kids we take in. Maybe later..."

"Well, you don't have to ask my permission—or even tell me. You can do anything you want to with the place." She turned her face away. "I've seen Grandpa's will. I'm not in it."

"Oh, Kate! I thought maybe you'd never have to find out."

She whirled to face him. "You thought I'd never find out? You knew? All this time, you knew I had no claim whatsoever on the place and you let me keep talking about *my* land? I'll bet you had fun with that one."

"Kate..." He tried to take her shoulders, but she jerked away.

"What else have you been trying to hide from me, *Dr.* Stephen Adams? Besides your wife and children?"

Steve grasped her shoulders, wanting to shake her—shake some sense into her. "What are you talking about, Kate? My wife and children?"

Kate gave him a stony glare. "Elizabeth. Freddy and Jody."

"Elizabeth? You think she's my *wife?* You think Freddy and Jody are my children? Elizabeth is my sister, Kate. Her kids are my niece and nephew. I've told you about Elizabeth. You met her at the theater with her husband, Fred, and his sister, Melissa."

"You told me your sister's name was Bet."

"Bet. Beth. Elizabeth. When I was a kid I couldn't say Elizabeth. I called her Bet. I still do sometimes."

"Oh."

He laughed and reached for Kate. She let him pull her into his arms. "How could I be married to someone else when I'm in love with you?"

She jerked back and looked at him. She fought to get out of his arms.

He let her go. *What's wrong now?*

"You love me? How can I believe *that* after all the lies you've told me?"

"Lies? What lies?"

"You didn't tell me you're a therapist. You didn't let me know I was left out of Grandpa's will. You purposely neglected to tell me about all the people coming to live here— and the schoolhouse you're going to build." She turned away. "I thought you were married and…"

"You *thought* I was married. I didn't say I was."

"You still tried to deceive me about all those other things."

"Why would I lie about loving you, Kate?" He reached for her.

She pushed him away. "I don't know why you said it. Maybe you think it will keep me from trying to find a loophole in Grandpa's will. I'm confused right now, Steve. I've got to have some time to sort out all this stuff you've thrown at me. If there's any sorting it out."

She whirled toward her car, feeling in a pocket of her slacks. She pulled out her car keys.

"Wait, Kate. Didn't you wear a coat?"

"I don't need it. I'm hot enough."

She climbed into the car and slammed the door. Then she opened it again. "Please tell your folks I'm not feeling well. You won't be lying this time. Bye, Steve."

Running a hand through his hair, he watched as she turned the car around and headed up the driveway. *Well, what do I do now? There's no figuring that woman out.* He looked up at the sky and prayed.

Chapter 21

On Monday morning, Steve sat in the rocker beside a dying fire in the fireplace, nursing his fifth cup of coffee for the day. He'd been too busy with the family all weekend to think much about what Kate had said to him on Saturday. But it was all he'd thought about since they'd left on Sunday evening.

Now it was Monday, he had tons of work to do and all he could think about was that stubborn female.

"Hotheaded redhead!" He dashed the remainder of his coffee into the hot ashes and heard them sizzle.

She had called him a liar. *A liar!*

He set the coffee mug on the hearth and stood. He couldn't sit around here all day brooding about it. He had work to do.

He ran his hand through his hair in frustration. *I guess I shouldn't have said I'm in love with her when she was so mad.* If he'd been thinking rationally, he wouldn't have. But she made him so angry he couldn't think straight, the way she jumped to conclusions, then refused to listen to reason.

He dropped back into the rocking chair, head between his hands, and massaged his scalp. Oh, the headaches that woman could give him.

He had been patient with her irrational behavior. He had smiled and spoken calmly and logically in the midst of her outbursts and it hadn't accomplished a thing.

Dr. Stephen Adams, she's not one of your patients.

His head came up. Where had that thought come from? Of course she was not his patient. He grinned to himself. If she was a patient, he'd already have her straightened out by now.

He wiped the grin from his face. Maybe she was not one of his patients, but hadn't he been trying to treat her like one? Like Kate said, he was looking at her as if she was just another case, another disturbed individual he needed to straighten out.

But he hadn't been thinking of her that way lately. His feelings for her were too personal.

Lowering his head, he closed his eyes, pressed his fingertips to his temples. *God, You know how often I pray about that woman. My prayers about her have been almost ceaseless since the day I met her.*

About her. Not for her, but about her? Frowning, he raised his head and opened his eyes. Maybe that was his trouble. He'd prayed a lot about her, but seldom had he actually prayed *for* her.

There was a difference, wasn't there?

Thinking about it, he had to admit he probably prayed for his clients more than he prayed for the woman he loved.

And how often had he told angry patients that it's difficult to stay angry with a person while praying for them? Maybe he should attend one of his own counseling sessions.

He must admit, too, he had prayed more about the way she was messing up his plans than he'd prayed for her. He really had not been fair to Kate. He should have told her a long time ago about his profession and his plans for the place.

I guess I was too big a coward, Lord. I'm sorry. If I can have one more chance…

He sat and talked to the Lord about it for a long time. Finally, he got to his feet smiling. He would give her a little time to cool off and then call her. If she wouldn't talk to him on the phone, he would go over to her uncle's house to see her—or to the law office if he had to.

He glanced around the room with a grin. Maybe he could entice her with a paintbrush and paint can. He would tear down the old wallpaper and get the walls ready to paint. He could pick up paint tomorrow on his way back from his afternoon sessions in Birmingham.

He worked diligently the remainder of the day taking down torn and faded wall covering and cleaning out dust and junk from behind it. Sorting the junk, he stopped, frowning at a paper in his hand. *What is this?*

He glanced at his watch. It was too late in the day to get into town and check it out. He would go in the morning before he left for Birmingham.

His business at the courthouse the next morning took much longer than he'd expected. Back at the house, he rushed to transfer file folders from the desk to his briefcase before heading out for his first appointment.

As he opened the front door to go out again, a gust of wind rattled papers he'd left lying on the desktop. He glanced back but continued out the door. He could take care of those later. Kate was the only one with a key and she was too riled at him to come over again so soon—if she ever came back at all.

Kate let herself into the house with the key Steve had given her. Yes, there was her jacket still hanging on the chair where Elizabeth—*his sister*—had hung it.

She stared at the almost-nude walls. *He's redoing the walls without me.*

It was a ridiculous thought—she hadn't seen him in ages and Saturday they'd fought. She walked to the rocking chair and plopped into it. Steve had said he didn't think the old house would be worth the effort or money it would take to restore it. Yet, when he'd seen what it meant to her, he'd begun work on it instead of working on his own project— the home for his parents and homeless children.

Maybe he really did love her as he said. And she had thrown his love back in his face by calling him a liar. How would she feel if he treated her in such a way? She had spent the weekend nurturing her anger at him and hadn't even considered his feelings. Now, sitting in the house where they had shared happy times together, she thought about his side of the situation.

Steve was not obligated to tell her about her grandfather's will.

When she'd asked if there was a Mrs. Steve Adams, he had not said there wasn't, so her overactive imagination had assumed there was.

He'd never made derogatory remarks about her chosen work as she'd made about his. He'd never referred to the gardening business as "playing in the dirt," the way her mother did. And when she continually berated him about the land, how could she blame him for failing to tell her about his plans for the place?

Could he ever forgive her? Would he even listen if she tried to tell him how sorry she was? What could she do to show him? She stood and looked around. Maybe she could begin by carrying the old wallpaper outside to be burned.

It looked as if the wind had scattered papers from the desk. She'd have to be careful not to gather up anything important with the stuff to burn.

She picked up a couple of papers, laid them on the desk-top and bent to pick up an old yellowed sheet.

Her mouth dropped open. What was this?

A deed?

And my name's on it!

She dropped into the desk chair staring. A deed made out to her by her grandfather, and witnessed by his old buddies who'd witnessed his will.

This is why he wanted me to take him to the county seat the day of his first stroke. To have it recorded.

Had her mother found it when she'd come by that evening and gotten his checkbook? When had she given it to Steve?

Kate's heart plummeted. Tears blinded her until she could barely read the land description. Or the note she wrote Steve.

Taking the deed, she ran to her car, leaving the front door standing open. She swiped at tears with dust-coated fingertips and started the car. She drove to the graveyard, parked at the foot of the hill and gazed at the marble head-stones shining in the sunlight.

Grandpa, forgive me. I was starting to blame you for everything that's gone wrong in my life. For Steve's coming here and making me fall in love with him so I wouldn't fight him about the land. For the loss of my hopes and dreams. Even for my quitting school.

And You, God. I blamed You for letting it all happen. Please forgive me.

With her arms and head propped on the steering wheel, she gave it all to Him—including the hurt over deception by Steve and her mother. And her grief over Steve not loving her.

No matter what someone else had or had not done, she had to do the right thing. She started the car and drove down the repaired driveway.

* * *

Steve stepped out of the pickup in front of the old farm-house and frowned. *I know I closed that door.* "Kate!" If she'd come while he was away… He dashed inside.

Her jacket was gone. And so was the deed. But a note lay on the desk. He picked it up and read, "Now I know why you said you love me."

Kate, Kate. He massaged his scalp. *What is this all about? Why do you always jump to conclusions?*

How would he ever make her believe him now?

He tried to call her but got no answer at her aunt's house or the attorney's office. Why did he not have her cell phone number?

Checking for his own phone, he headed for the woods. Maybe she had gone to the old campsite, now his build-ing site.

He glanced around the clearing, looked up in the limbs of her favorite tree, checked the stream and tried calling her office and uncle's house again. No Kate.

Propping a stick of firewood against a tree, he sat down and massaged his temples.

When bushes rattled nearby, his head shot up, his eyes flew open.

Kate stood before him, a streak of sunlight setting her short curls ablaze.

He willed himself to be calm. "Hello, Katie."

She held out a paper and moved closer. "I brought the deed back. No one else has to know about it, so you can go ahead with your building plans. I think Grandpa would have liked what you're doing with the place."

She said it in a rush like a memorized speech she wanted to get out before forgetting what she planned to say. She shook the paper at him. "Here. Take it. This is already hard enough."

He shook his head. "It's been recorded in your name."

She frowned and looked at the folded paper. "I didn't see anyplace where it was stamped."

"How closely did you look at it?"

She shrugged. "I looked at it. But it doesn't matter. A lawyer can fix things so it's legally yours."

"Look again."

She unfolded the paper and turned it sideways. He watched her lips move as she read the stamping in the margin. Her frown increased. "It was recorded today. Before I saw it. Before I knew it existed. How...? Why...?"

Steve's heart pounded in his chest as he waited for her to figure it out. He couldn't lose his cool now. He leaned back against the tree. "I'm sorry if I got dust on your jacket when I ripped down that torn wallpaper behind the desk. You should have seen all the stuff flying out from behind there. An old check written by your grandfather. A—"

"You found it today behind the wallpaper! You found the deed and Grandpa's check to the gas company. He knocked them behind the desk and into that big torn place when he had the stroke and fell. You had it recorded before you knew I'd seen it. Oh, Steve!"

He barely got his arms open in time to catch her as she dove at him. Still, she knocked him off his makeshift stool—just like the day he'd met her. Only this time, from the look on her face, she wasn't angry with him.

Both were on the ground, he on his back, she on top of him.

He wrapped his arms around her. "There you go, knocking me off my stool again."

She laughed. "It got me into your arms, didn't it?"

Epilogue

A year later, on a beautiful spring morning, the house stood white and stately in the sunlight. A lush, green lawn swept from the house to the edge of the woodland. Steve stood beside an archway entwined with roses and sweet-smelling honeysuckle that marked a path through the trees.

Dogwood trees in full bloom rivaled the brilliance of Kate's long white gown as she glided across the grass toward him. But Kate knew by the expression on his face that nothing could compete for him with the glorious red cloud—as he called it—surrounding her glowing face and sparkling green-and-gold-flecked eyes.

During the previous year, while she'd finished earning her horticulture and art degrees and Steve had restored the old farmhouse and supervised the building of a home for his parents and the boys, Kate's hair had grown long again. At his request, she wore only a crown of flowers on her head, and no veil covering her hair.

Even her mother glowed with pride as she stood beside

the flower-decked arch holding the matron-of-honor bouquet and waiting for her younger daughter to glide across the grassy carpet on her father's arm. She didn't even frown when Kate stubbed her toe just as she reached the archway—and fell into Steve's arms.

The preacher cleared his throat. The adult guests gasped. The children—Amy as the flower girl, little Tommy holding the ring, Mama and Papa Ad's boys as Steve's groomsmen—giggled.

Steve spoke close to Kate's ear. "Still falling for me, are you?"

Kate stifled her own giggle. "Always, now and forever."

Steve gave her a little squeeze and set her firmly on her feet.

"Who gives this woman to be married to this man?"

Kate's father looked at the preacher. "Her mother and I," he said.

And, in Kate's heart, she heard loud and clear: *I know the plans I have for you, plans to give you a future and a hope.*

* * * * *

REQUEST YOUR FREE BOOKS!

2 FREE CHRISTIAN NOVELS
PLUS 2
FREE
MYSTERY GIFTS

HEARTSONG
PRESENTS

REQUEST YOUR FREE BOOKS!

2 FREE INSPIRATIONAL NOVELS
PLUS 2
FREE
MYSTERY GIFTS

Love Inspired
HISTORICAL
INSPIRATIONAL HISTORICAL ROMANCE

YES! Please send me 2 FREE Love Inspired® Historical novels and my 2 FREE mystery gifts (gifts are worth about $10). After receiving them, if I don't wish to receive any more books, I can return the shipping statement marked "cancel." If I don't cancel, I will receive 4 brand-new novels every month and be billed just $4.74 per book in the U.S. or $5.24 per book in Canada. That's a savings of at least 21% off the cover price. It's quite a bargain! Shipping and handling is just 50¢ per book in the U.S. and 75¢ per book in Canada.* I understand that accepting the 2 free books and gifts places me under no obligation to buy anything. I can always return a shipment and cancel at any time. Even if I never buy another book, the two free books and gifts are mine to keep forever.

102/302 IDN F5CY

Name _____ (PLEASE PRINT)

Address _____ Apt. #

City _____ State/Prov. _____ Zip/Postal Code

Signature (if under 18, a parent or guardian must sign)

Mail to the Harlequin® Reader Service:
IN U.S.A.: P.O. Box 1867, Buffalo, NY 14240-1867
IN CANADA: P.O. Box 609, Fort Erie, Ontario L2A 5X3

Want to try two free books from another series?
Call 1-800-873-8635 or visit www.ReaderService.com.

* Terms and prices subject to change without notice. Prices do not include applicable taxes. Sales tax applicable in N.Y. Canadian residents will be charged applicable taxes. Offer not valid in Quebec. This offer is limited to one order per household. Not valid for current subscribers to Love Inspired Historical books. All orders subject to credit approval. Credit or debit balances in a customer's account(s) may be offset by any other outstanding balance owed by or to the customer. Please allow 4 to 6 weeks for delivery. Offer available while quantities last.

Your Privacy—The Harlequin® Reader Service is committed to protecting your privacy. Our Privacy Policy is available online at www.ReaderService.com or upon request from the Harlequin Reader Service.

We make a portion of our mailing list available to reputable third parties that offer products we believe may interest you. If you prefer that we not exchange your name with third parties, or if you wish to clarify or modify your communication preferences, please visit us at www.ReaderService.com/consumerchoice or write to us at Harlequin Reader Service Preference Service, P.O. Box 9062, Buffalo, NY 14269. Include your complete name and address.

LIHDIR13R

REQUEST YOUR FREE BOOKS!

2 FREE INSPIRATIONAL NOVELS
PLUS 2
FREE
MYSTERY GIFTS

Love Inspired

YES! Please send me 2 FREE Love Inspired® novels and my 2 FREE mystery gifts (gifts are worth about $10). After receiving them, if I don't wish to receive any more books, I can return the shipping statement marked "cancel." If I don't cancel, I will receive 6 brand-new novels every month and be billed just $4.74 per book in the U.S. or $5.24 per book in Canada. That's a savings of at least 21% off the cover price. It's quite a bargain! Shipping and handling is just 50¢ per book in the U.S. and 75¢ per book in Canada.* I understand that accepting the 2 free books and gifts places me under no obligation to buy anything. I can always return a shipment and cancel at any time. Even if I never buy another book, the two free books and gifts are mine to keep forever.

105/305 IDN F49N

Name	(PLEASE PRINT)
Address	Apt. #
City	State/Prov. Zip/Postal Code

Signature (if under 18, a parent or guardian must sign)

Mail to the Harlequin® Reader Service:
IN U.S.A.: P.O. Box 1867, Buffalo, NY 14240-1867
IN CANADA: P.O. Box 609, Fort Erie, Ontario L2A 5X3

**Are you a subscriber to Love Inspired books
and want to receive the larger-print edition?
Call 1-800-873-8635 or visit www.ReaderService.com.**

* Terms and prices subject to change without notice. Prices do not include applicable taxes. Sales tax applicable in N.Y. Canadian residents will be charged applicable taxes. Offer not valid in Quebec. This offer is limited to one order per household. Not valid for current subscribers to Love Inspired books. All orders subject to credit approval. Credit or debit balances in a customer's account(s) may be offset by any other outstanding balance owed by or to the customer. Please allow 4 to 6 weeks for delivery. Offer available while quantities last.

Your Privacy—The Harlequin® Reader Service is committed to protecting your privacy. Our Privacy Policy is available online at www.ReaderService.com or upon request from the Harlequin Reader Service.
We make a portion of our mailing list available to reputable third parties that offer products we believe may interest you. If you prefer that we not exchange your name with third parties, or if you wish to clarify or modify your communication preferences, please visit us at www.ReaderService.com/consumerchoice or write to us at Harlequin Reader Service Preference Service, P.O. Box 9062, Buffalo, NY 14269. Include your complete name and address.

LIDIR13R